Giving in

to Gravity

by Avery Bridge

Edited by Maureen Cooke
Cover art by Crystal at magicbookcoverdesign.com

About This Book

Riley O'Brien identifies as nonbinary and uses they/him pronouns. The other characters refer to them using he/him pronouns, except their mother who misgenders them using she/her pronouns.

CONTENT WARNING: brief descriptions of misgendering by a parent.

This story represents an idealized depiction of coming out in the year 2000. In many ways it is what I wished it had been like for my friends and myself, and what I hope it might be like going forward. I recognize that every LGBTQ+ person's experience is unique. I am not attempting to suggest that this is the way every nonbinary or queer person expresses themselves. This is simply my idea of what it could have been like for two people who found each other when they needed them the most.

Song List

I hope you enjoy this playlist that inspired me while writing *Giving in to Gravity* Songs mentioned in the book are listed in **BOLD**

1. "Graduate" Third Eye Blind
2. "Fly Away" Lenny Kravitz
3. "When I Come Around" Green Day
4. "Anthem for the Year 2000" Silverchair
5. "We Are the Normal" Goo Goo Dolls
6. "Satellite" Dave Matthews Band
7. "Dammit" Blink-182
8. "Real World" Matchbox Twenty
9. "Kryptonite" 3 Doors Down
10. **"Everything You Want" Vertical Horizon**
11. "Good" Better Than Ezra
12. "Just Watch the Fireworks" Jimmy Eat World
13. **"Motorcycle Drive By" Third Eye Blind**
14. "Secret Smile" Semisonic

15. "I Want You" Savage Garden
16. "Everlong" Foo Fighters
17. "Wonderwall" Oasis
18. "Mad Season" Matchbox Twenty
19. "One More Time" Daft Punk
20. "Here's to the Night" Eve 6
21. "Save Tonight" Eagle-Eye Cherry
22. "Glycerine" Bush
23. "Good Riddance(Time of Your Life)" Green Day
24. "Stellar" Incubus
25. "Slide" Goo Goo Dolls
26. "If You're Gone" Matchbox Twenty
27. "I'll Be" Edwin McCain

For anyone who is still

finding themself

One

Riley

Riley watched from their window as the mail truck parked in front of the cluster box across the street. They hurried to the front door, bouncing on the balls of their feet until they saw the truck drive away. As they rushed down the sidewalk, the spring wind whipped their freshly-dyed green hair around their face.

Their breath caught in their throat when they opened the mailbox and saw the large white envelope. It was addressed to Riley-Anne O'Brien and embossed with a shiny red "T." They had been expecting their acceptance letter to New Mexico Tech, and a large envelope was always a good sign. They pulled it out

gingerly, cradling it in one arm
while they scooped up the rest of the
mail. Riley's mind was already racing
ahead toward their future plans. The
next four years living on their own
studying computer science were going
to be awesome. But once they got back
inside the house and looked more
closely at the insignia, their
elation turned instantly into dread.

It was a registration packet
for Torrance Academy, the
college-immersion boot camp their
stepdad Hank was forcing them to
attend. All they wanted to do was
graduate high school and then hole up
in their room playing *Diablo II* until
college, but Hank had other plans.
Riley's heart started pounding as
panic crawled up their spine. The
thought of spending eight whole weeks
at a girls' boarding school learning
how to write a thesis and pledge a
sorority made them want to ralph.

Riley plopped the stack of mail onto the kitchen table and took the envelope to their room. They hesitated inside their door, holding the packet above the waste basket. Maybe if they threw it away they wouldn't have to go? Deep down they knew that would never work; Hank would just call and have the school send another one when he realized it hadn't been filled out. Riley couldn't wait until August, when they would finally turn eighteen and be out from under his thumb once and for all.

Wanting a distraction, Riley sank into their desk chair and booted up their computer. But while they waited for the dial-up to connect, their eyes kept glancing over to the envelope on their desk. With a resigned sigh, they sliced it open and pulled out the registration form. The first thing they did was fill out their name correctly: Riley O'Brien, *not* Riley-Anne like it was addressed to. The rest was simple enough until they came to the checkbox labeled *male* or *female*. It was only ever those two choices. Riley frowned deeply, wondering what would happen if they simply did not check either one.

Then they were struck by a wild idea. Thumbing through the brochure that came with the packet, they double-checked that Torrance did in fact also have a boys' school on the same campus as the girls'. Before they could over-think their decision, they penned a decisive "x" into the box labeled *male*. It still didn't feel quite right, but compared to the idea of *female* it was a vast improvement. Riley finished filling out the rest of the form with ease, sealed the return envelope, and walked back outside to slide it into the outgoing mailbox. If they were going to spend their summer in

purgatory, at least they were going
to do it their way.

Two

Sebastian

Sebastian Otero sat on the roof of Torrance Academy, his feet dangling over the edge as he watched all of the new students arrive on campus for their acclaimed pre-college immersion program. It was a tradition he had made for himself ever since his father had accepted the position of Dean of Students six years ago, and had moved the two of them into the cottage behind the school. The only difference this summer was that Sebastian, as a newly minted high school graduate, was now one of them.

The midmorning sun glinted off of the pond in the center of the campus, complete with an obstacle ropes course in the middle of it. Sebastian had been practicing on the course in between every session for as long as he had lived there, getting ready for the day when it would be his turn. His imagination overflowed with images of himself finally joining in, instead of watching from the sidelines. More students were arriving now, finding a place to sit on the lawn or claiming a bench in the quad.

As he watched, he noticed a motorcycle heading up the back road toward the school. Intrigued, he moved around to the north side of the roof to get a better look. The driver parked the bike in a secluded spot, looking around to see if anyone had spotted them. Of course they never thought to glance up toward Sebastian's hiding place. After a moment, they took their helmet off and shook out their unruly, neon-green hair. They stashed their helmet next to the bike, shouldered their backpack, and pushed their way through the brush toward the front of the school.

Sebastian had never met anyone who drove a motorcycle, or had hair that vibrant. He had lived on this school campus since he was twelve, being homeschooled by his dad and barely leaving except to go into the tiny town of Glorieta for groceries. The groups of students who attended all of the pre-college programs had always been older than him, and left before he even learned their names.

But if he had his own motorcycle... Sebastian closed his eyes, the backs of the lids bright red in the brilliant sunshine. He could envision all the places he would get to explore if he had a motorcycle. He thought about what it would be like to only be accountable to himself: no school, no pressure, no responsibilities. Just him and the open road. It sounded like freedom. Sebastian jumped up from his vantage point and rushed downstairs: he had to find the owner of the bike.

By the time Sebastian reached the main entrance of the school, there was no sign of the motorcyclist. People were milling around all over the grounds: they could be anywhere. They could be anyone at all. He didn't even know if they were a student, although he couldn't imagine any of the faculty rocking that hair color. He decided instead to go get a better look at the bike itself.

Torrance Academy was on the outskirts of Glorieta, New Mexico- a collection of buildings that could barely be called a town- nestled in the Sangre de Cristo mountains. The campus occupied a clearing that consisted of a large pond in the center with many tall brick buildings all around it. Dense forest surrounded the clearing in every direction, evergreens teeming with wildlife year round.

Sebastian trekked all the way to the north edge of the grounds where he had seen the driver park the bike. It was propped up behind a large boulder, and clearly visible from the road. The motorcycle was a beautiful machine, all black leather and chrome. His dad would be furious if he found out that Sebastian had always wanted one. Dean Otero was staunchly opposed to anything even remotely dangerous. Sebastian strengthened his resolve to find the owner and ask them where they had gotten it.

He looked around, making sure he was alone, then swung a leg over to sit astride the bike. Sebastian gripped the throttle in his right hand, imagining how it would feel to race down the mountain pass, wind in his hair. A loud noise off to his left startled him, and he jumped off the motorcycle just in time to see the groundskeeper rounding the corner with a weed wacker.

He did his best to camouflage the bike in the surrounding scrub brush, but it would still be visible to anyone who walked this way.

Then he squared his shoulders and approached the groundskeeper.

"Hey Bob!" Sebastian waved an arm in greeting.

"Sebastian!" Bob powered down the trimmer and smiled at him. "Excited for your first day?"

"You know it!" He put a hand on Bob's shoulder, subtly turning him away from the motorcycle. "You've been working overtime all weekend getting the place ready for the summer session, and it looks great. How does a break sound? My dad has drinks and stuff set up in the gym."

Bob nodded gratefully, wiping his brow as they walked together back toward the school. Sebastian sighed with relief. He didn't know why the driver of the motorcycle had decided to hide it back here instead of parking it in the student lot, and until he figured it out he was determined to help them keep it a secret. The bike was safe for the moment, but he needed to secure a better hiding spot for it as soon as possible.

Three

Riley

Riley tried to keep their breathing under control as they made their way to the registrar's office of Torrance Academy. They joined the river of students passing beneath the *Welcome Class of 2000* banner, glancing furtively from side to side trying to gauge if anyone was paying them any attention. So far so good, but this was only the first step. The imposing brick facade towered in front of them, looking more like a castle than any building in a small town in New Mexico had a right to. Part college prep-school, part boot camp, this was the last place Riley would have chosen to spend the summer after high school. But since they didn't have a choice, at least they had figured out a way to be here on their own terms. Riley noticed the boys who were in line in front of them branching off toward the walk-up window on the right side of the office, labeled *Torrance Academy for Boys,* and followed suit.

They gave their name to the clerk and waited anxiously as she scanned her list for them. What if the registration hadn't gone through? What if someone had noticed that they checked the other box, assumed it was a mistake and switched them over to the girls' school? After what felt like an eternity, she crossed their name off of her list. Then she handed them a copy of their registration form to sign. When they saw their name at the top, Riley O'Brien instead of Riley-Anne, they felt a bit more hopeful. The box next to *male* was still marked with an 'x', and they began to relax a little.

"School ID photo station is right inside, keep your ID with you at all times," She instructed. "Welcome packets are in the gymnasium, orientation is at twelve o'clock sharp."

The largest building housed the gymnasium, cafeteria, library, and administration offices. The inside featured soaring ceilings with high windows, and a large staircase directly ahead. Hallways branched off to the left and right. Riley followed the signs directing them down the left hall, first to the ID photo station and then to the gym entrance.

Inside the gym, tables were set up in a row with large letters hanging off of the front of each one. Riley wandered toward the table marked "K - O."

"O'Brien," they handed over the ID that had just been printed for them.

"Riley," The volunteer rifled through her stack of folders and then nodded. "Here you are." She pulled their folder out of the pile and handed it to them. It had a key taped to the front.

"Your class schedule, map, dorm assignment, and school rules. Welcome to Torrance!" She handed them a cloth bag full of Torrance merchandise.

"Thank you." *This place must be costing Hank a fortune,* Riley thought with a bit of satisfaction. A line was beginning to form as more students filed into the gym. Riley was gathering up all of their things when someone spoke quietly right behind them.

"I know your secret."

"Wha-what?" Riley's heart hammered against their sternum and blood roared in their ears. Someone had figured it out. They were already caught. Their hands trembled so badly they almost dropped all the papers, but managed to stuff them into the tote just in time. They turned around to face their accuser. He was another student, slightly taller than Riley, with artfully tousled black hair and deep brown eyes. The epitome of clean-cut, he wore a crisp Torrance Academy polo shirt and khaki shorts.

"I saw your motorcycle," he told them, still keeping his voice low. "You didn't hide it very well. Why did you leave it out there, anyway?"

Riley blew out a breath, feeling lightheaded as relief flooded their body. This was just about the bike. "None of your business."

"Listen, you could really use some help in this situation. An ally. Someone who knows the ins and outs of this place."

"And that someone should be you?"

"I have connections high up," he insisted. "Seriously, no one else knows their way around Torrance like I do. You need me."

"What do you get out of it?" Riley wondered.

"Maybe a ride or two on the bike?"

Riley narrowed their eyes at him. Was this guy for real?

"I'm not a narc, I swear." He held up both hands. "I'm Sebastian, by the way."

"Riley."

"Otero," Sebastian leaned past Riley to hand his ID to the volunteer at the table. "Just think about it, Riley." Sebastian collected his folder and bag, then headed off to join a group of guys in the bleachers waiting for orientation to start. Riley sat alone, arms crossed as they pondered everything Sebastian had said.

Finally the gym quieted as a man stepped up to the podium that had been set up in the middle of the basketball court. Riley yawned, already feeling boredom poking at the edges of their mind.

"Welcome class of 2000!" the man exclaimed into the microphone. "I am Mr. Otero, Dean of Students at Torrance Academy for Boys." Riley's head snapped up as he recognized the name. The same name Sebastian had just given to the registration volunteer. "I'm so happy to welcome you all here for our immersive pre-college program. We have a really special summer planned out for you, so I hope you all brought your A-game."

Riley tuned him out, wishing they had thought to bring their Game Boy.

"At Torrance Academy, we strive to provide you with the full college experience, to prepare you to enter the collegiate world with your best foot forward. In service of that interest, we have academic classes

that rival the best college
prep-schools in the country, as well
as a rigorous physical education
program to keep you in tip-top shape.
Lastly, one of the most important
aspects of any higher education plan
is making social contacts. The
friends you meet here could end up
being the people you count on for the
rest of your life. We have numerous
activities to choose from, to suit
any interest or talent. Sign up
sheets will be posted in the hallway
outside the office, and let it be
known that participation is
mandatory. Now here's the pep squad
with a performance for you!"

Riley ducked out of the gym
just before the opening notes of
"Jock Jams Megamix" blasted out of
the speakers. They couldn't believe
they were stuck here for the entire
summer. They exited the main building
and, following the map they found in

their folder, turned right toward the boys' dormitory.

They held their breath as they entered, still convinced that someone was about to grab them and insist that they're not allowed to be here. But there wasn't a soul in sight as they climbed the stairs to the second floor. Even so, it wasn't until they had found their room, slipped inside, and locked the door behind them that they were able to relax.

The idea of spending an entire summer at a girls' boarding school, having to dress up and pretend every moment of every day, was their absolute worst nightmare. But when the paperwork came to the house, all it took was one little checkmark next to the box labeled *male*. It was the first step toward living the life they had always envisioned for themself, but they had never dreamed they would actually make it here. And now, printed in bold calligraphy on

the folder they held in their hands,
were the words *Riley O'Brien -veritas
est virtus- Torrance Academy for Boys*.
Riley stared at the words, and then
slowly a grin spread over their face.

They had made it.

Four

Riley

"Hey Mom," Riley spoke into the answering machine. "I'm just calling to let you know I'm here at Torrance, I got registered and I'm settling into my room. Wish me luck!"

They hung up the payphone that stood just outside the main school building. They hadn't really expected her to answer; she was rarely at home. Even this many miles away, they still felt like they were lying by not telling her they had enrolled at the boys' school. They would figure out a way to tell her eventually, but it was never going to happen if she didn't pick up the phone. Maybe it was better this way. They might not be able to reach her while they were up here, but if they couldn't talk to

each other then they couldn't fight
with each other. Always a bright
side.

The next day, summer classes
began at Torrance. Riley took care
getting ready, wanting to look just
right. It was easier than expected:
no makeup to apply, no curling iron,
no uncomfortable heels. The hardest
part was wrapping their chest tightly
with an ace bandage. After that it
was just sneakers, baggy shorts, and
a loose t-shirt with the Torrance
insignia. When they looked in the
mirror, a feeling of *rightness* washed
over them. A backwards black Adidas
hat to tame messy green hair was the
finishing touch, and Riley was out
the door. For the first time ever,
they felt like themself.

According to their paperwork,
their first cohort meeting was out on
the dock by the pond. Strange place
for class, but Riley shrugged and
jogged across the grounds, glad they

had managed to leave on time this morning. They arrived to find most of the guys already there, laughing and rough-housing by the water. Riley hung back in the shade of a tree, looking for the teacher. This wasn't how any of their other schools had conducted class, and it was a little disconcerting. The summer sun was stifling, and Riley was already sweating.

"I've been wondering,"

Riley startled at the sound of a voice behind them, then turned around. Sebastian had once again managed to sneak up on them, just like yesterday.

"How'd you manage to get a motorcycle like that?"

"I had just finished making a delivery for work when I ran out of gas." Riley shrugged, trying to seem nonchalant. "I stopped at a station and as I'm filling up I look across the street and there it is. Just sitting there with a for-sale sign. The back of the delivery truck was empty, I had all this cash in my pocket from the sale, so I walked over and bought it."

"You bought it with the cash you just made on your work delivery?" Sebastian's eyebrows shot up.

"Yeah, well, my boss was a jackass." Riley bristled, feeling defensive. "He's also my stepdad, so pissing him off was just an added bonus."

"Oh, damn!" Sebastian whistled. "Already taking down The Man. Impressive."

"Not so impressive now, though. Got me sentenced here for the summer. I had to bring the bike with me; he'd have sold it right out from under me if I left it behind. He might try to track it down up here - that's why I stashed it. How'd you even know about it, anyway?"

"I have my ways. I told you, I have this place wired."

"If I let you hide it somewhere else, you have to promise not to tell anyone about it."

"I'm like a vault," Sebastian placed a hand over his heart. "I can keep a secret."

He was looking at Riley with such a hopeful expression that they couldn't help but soften a little. "Can you?" Riley wanted to trust him, but knew from experience that that was a dangerous thing to want.

"Afternoon, gentlemen!" The teacher finally arrived and called the class to begin.

Five

Sebastian

Sebastian joined the rest of the guys outside for homeroom, feeling elated that he had found the owner of the motorcycle so quickly. It hadn't been difficult at all, considering Riley turned out to be the only person on campus with green hair. He was confident that he would be driving the bike himself in no time, and the prospect filled him with excitement.

"My name is Lincoln," the teacher went on. "No 'mister', just Lincoln. I'll be your cohort leader for the summer. Consider me your drill sergeant, but also your literature professor and your counselor. You can come to me with anything, big or small, I'm here for you." And with that he walked right into the pond, fully clothed. The boys erupted into laughter. Sebastian grinned, having seen this trick from afar every summer and feeling like he was in on an inside joke. "What are you waiting for? First one to the boat gets a free pass from drills this morning!"

The laughter turned into raucous cheering, and Sebastian got swept up in the moment as he raced the other guys to the boat tethered to the far side of the obstacle course. He plunged into the cold pond, pulling himself through the water with confident strokes. The first obstacle was a rough-spun rope ladder dangling from the wooden beam above them that spanned the pond to the main structure in the center. From the middle of the beam hung a swinging rope looped around a hook at the top of the ladder.

Sebastian grasped the first rung of the ladder and started pulling himself upward. It bowed and twisted under his weight and he almost fell off a couple of times before he reached the swinging rope. He swung across the water to land on the lowest platform of the climbing wall, then turned to swing the rope back toward the guy who had clambered onto the ladder after him. Next he scrambled up the side of the tower as fast as he could. He could hear someone right behind him and pushed himself faster. From the top, he took a zipline across the other side of the pond, landing on the dock next to a small motor boat. Lincoln blew the whistle that hung around his neck, signaling the end of the race.

Once inside the boat, Sebastian finally turned and looked back to see who was trailing him. It was one of the guys he had met yesterday at orientation, Ben Rodriguez. Ben reached the boat a few seconds too late. All of his practice sessions had paid off, and Sebastian relaxed into the boat with his feet up on the seat across from him. Ben cursed and flopped down onto the dock to catch his breath.

"Damn, you're fast," Ben acknowledged. More of the guys were landing on the dock now, joining Ben where he lay sprawled. The rest were laughing and splashing as they tried to climb over each other onto the ladder before deciding to just bypass the tower and swim across the pond instead. Riley brought up the rear, green hair now a darker shade after being submerged in the water.

Once everyone had reached the dock, Lincoln blew his whistle again and instructed them all to run laps around the pond. When this announcement was met with a chorus of groans, he blew the whistle loudly in quick succession until each of them were on their feet jogging. Then he joined Sebastian in the boat and started the motor.

Sebastian enjoyed the wind on his face as the boat skimmed across the water. He felt as if his whole life had been building toward this moment, and now he was living the experience instead of just watching from the sidelines. It was finally his turn.

Six

Riley

Riley, who had never been much for aerobic exercise, found themself trailing behind their cohort as they were all forced to run laps around the pond. Aside from the compulsory cardio, school seemed to be going okay so far. None of the guys except Sebastian had spoken to them yet, but no one was giving them any suspicious side-eye either. Meanwhile, Lincoln cruised along beside them in what looked like a motorized fishing boat, asking them questions. Sebastian waved at all of them from his seat in Lincoln's boat, kicking back in a show of relaxation. *This must be some kind of cruel and unusual punishment*, Riley lamented as their lungs burned and thighs ached.

"Who was the greatest writer in history?" Lincoln called out from his megaphone.

"Faulkner!" someone immediately yelled. Sebastian visibly blanched at this answer.

"Wrong!" Lincoln shouted. "The correct answer is, there is no right answer!" Everyone laughed. "Remember, I am not just here to whip you into shape, but to teach you how to think for yourselves. Like Faulkner, or Fitzgerald. Hemingway and Steinbeck. What did these writers all have in common?"

They were all white dudes? Riley wanted to shout back but held their tongue.

"They forged their own paths."

Riley rolled their eyes. Of course this class was going to be a misogynistic hero-worship romp. Heaven forbid they open up a Virginia Woolf or Alice Walker. They decided to tune him out and concentrate on not passing out, wishing they hadn't fastened their binder quite so tightly this morning.

As soon as class ended Riley made a beeline back to their dorm room. They couldn't wait to get out of their sticky clothes and shower. They left their door open as they shoved clean clothes and toiletries into their backpack, ready to turn right back around and go scope out some less-frequented shower options. When they did, they almost ran right into Sebastian as he was walking past their door.

"Hey," he stepped into their room.

"Just come on in, why don't you," Riley grumbled, already feeling annoyed at being delayed.

"Sorry," Sebastian backed up with exaggerated steps, then knocked loudly on the doorframe. "Permission to come aboard, sir?" He imitated a British accent.

"Granted."

"How the hell did you score a single room?" He sounded impressed as he strode around the small room.

"Oh please," Riley snorted. "That was nothing. I just hacked into the school's database and made sure I got assigned a single. Piece of cake."

"It's not nothing," Sebastian insisted. "Everyone else here would kill to have their own room."

"Don't you have your own room in the Dean's house, *Otero*?" Riley stared intently at him, watching his reaction. Sebastian flinched.

"How do you know where I live?"

"Lucky guess."

Sebastian's eyes narrowed. "What else did you find out about me, hacker?"

"Only child of Dean Otero, homeschooled, accepted to UNM's biology undergrad program." Riley rattled off. "Let's just say you're

not the only one who has this place
'wired'."

"Noted." Sebastian looked
uncomfortable, but not angry.

"Want to see the intake files
for the other guys?" Riley offered.

"You're on." Sebastian seemed
to relax as Riley opened their lime
green iBook and pulled up the school
database. Once Riley had gotten into
the database to double-check their
room assignment, it was easy enough
to snoop around. Their curiosity had
gotten the better of them and they
had spent their first night reading
up on the students they would be
spending the summer with.

As they watched Sebastian
peruse the forbidden files, another
thought suddenly occurred to them.
Sebastian might immediately alert his
father about Riley's computer
hacking, and if they got sent home
early it would be no skin off their
back. Hank would be pissed, but that

was pretty much his natural state anyways. On the other hand, if Sebastian didn't rat them out for this transgression, maybe they would be able to trust him with their motorcycle after all.

When Sebastian left, Riley hurried to resume their quest for a private shower. They pulled their backpack full of clothes and toiletries onto their shoulders and left the dorm. There was only one other place they could think of that might work.

The gym was empty as most students gathered in the cafeteria for dinner. Through a back door, Riley found the solution to their conundrum: the locker rooms were equipped with shower stalls. Just like in high school, everyone eschewed these showers in favor of the ones inside the dorm building. Riley luxuriated in the hot water, eager to wash away the sweat and

grime left behind after their
exhausting first class.

Now clean and redressed, Riley
was walking past the main office when
they saw Sebastian posting a sign-up
sheet under the mandatory activities
board. Curious, Riley stepped forward
to get a closer look. If they had to
sign up for something, at least they
could join a group with someone they
already kind of knew. They waited
until Sebastian left and then signed
their name at the top of the page.

"Oh, you play polo?" Sebastian
suddenly reappeared at the board.

"Polo?" Riley repeated, looking
back at the flier they had just
written their name on. Sure enough,
it was the Torrance Academy Polo Club
they had just signed up for. "Well,
actually-"

"We play arena polo, which is a
bit different from what you might be
used to." Sebastian continued talking
excitedly. "It's a much smaller

field, so we have to be a lot more precise. And it's three to a side instead of four."

"That sounds…cool." Riley was nodding as if they had any idea what Sebastian was talking about.

"It's a lot of fun, I'm glad you'll be joining us."

Sebastian was smiling at them so earnestly that Riley couldn't bring themself to change their mind. No one had ever wanted Riley on their team before.

"Me too," Riley smiled back, feeling warmth spreading from their toes all the way up to their ears. *Guess I'll be learning to play polo this summer,* Riley thought. *Maybe it won't be so bad.*

After grabbing a quick bite to eat, Riley headed back to their room where they closed and locked the door. They kicked their flip flops into the closet along with their shorts and T-shirt. Last, they unwrapped their chest binder and threw it onto the laundry pile. Riley flopped backward onto their bed, taking a deep breath and relishing the feeling of full lung expansion that was never quite possible while wearing a binder. In spite of the forced exertion this morning, they thought it had gone pretty well. No one had accused them of being in the wrong place. They had joined a club, possibly made a friend, and most importantly they had survived their first day.

Seven

Sebastian

The first week of school flew by in a blur. Sebastian was already having the time of his life, competing against the other guys in the cohort to see who could run the fastest around the pond or who could answer the most questions about literature. It usually ended up being either Ben or Sebastian to win the race, and then Ben or Riley to answer the most questions. Sebastian was just waiting for the day when Ben would win both at the same time. Lincoln had promised to award anyone who accomplished it an entire day off.

Friday afternoon rolled around, and Sebastian held the first polo practice in the gym. He wanted to show the guys the rules of play on foot before they would attempt it on horseback. Ben showed up, along with his roommate Scott Carter. When more guys from Lincoln's class arrived, he recognized Adam, Tyler, and Jon. The others were from different cohorts and Sebastian went to introduce himself. Lastly he saw Riley hesitating in the doorway.

"Okay everybody, huddle up!" Sebastian called out, waiting until everyone clustered around him. "Welcome to the Torrance Academy polo club!" He had a bag of hockey sticks and a rubber ball in front of him. He doled out one stick to each player and instructed them to divide into two teams. Then he had them practice rotating in and out of positions one, two and three, passing the ball back and forth across the court. "Arena polo is an equal opportunity sport, there's no quarterback. I need each of you to be able to swap into any position at any time, so learn them all."

When he felt they all had a pretty good handle on the positions, he started running them through some drills. Then he noticed that Riley was continually hanging back and not really participating.

"Something wrong, O'Brien?"

"I just, uh," Riley stammered. "I've never really played a team sport before. Or ridden a horse."

"Oh man, I should've put on the flier that basic horsemanship skills are required." Sebastian hung his head. "I guess I thought it was kind of implied? I can give you lessons if you want, but you wouldn't be ready to compete this summer."

"Oh no, I definitely don't want lessons." Riley hurriedly declined, green eyes widening in fear.

"So...why did you sign up for the polo club?" Sebastian was finding it hard to believe that someone who drove a motorcycle could actually be afraid to ride a horse, but anything's possible.

"Honestly, I just sorta picked the first club I saw. I'm not exactly a joiner, but the Dean said it was mandatory."

"Listen, we still need a timekeeper if you want to give it a shot." Sebastian suggested, but Riley still looked skeptical. "No horseback riding required, I promise."

Riley nodded, and Sebastian handed over his stopwatch while explaining how to time each seven-minute period, or chukka, and when to blow the whistle. Something about Riley had reminded Sebastian of himself, always watching from the sidelines and never able to join in. He wanted to make sure no one ever felt left out.

That weekend, Sebastian was bumming around the dorms just happy that he was finally allowed to hang out there. The common room was a large lounge area with a fireplace set into one wall, and a big-screen

TV in the corner with a semicircle of couches facing it. The opposite wall featured a table and chairs next to a fridge with a microwave on top. He saw Ben watching TV and sank down into the brown leather couch next to him. He was flipping through the same five channels over and over, not stopping at any of them. From what Sebastian could tell, the only choices were infomercials or *Jerry Springer*. He almost offered to invite Ben to his house to watch cable, but he tried to avoid reminding people that he was the son of the Dean.

Then Scott appeared in the doorway. "You guys up for a game?" he asked them, twirling a basketball on one finger. Sebastian and Ben immediately followed him outside. Adam, Tyler, and Jon saw them heading toward the court and soon they had a game of 3-on-3. They played until the burning rays of summer sun forced them back indoors.

There was still nothing to watch, so one of the guys suggested they head over to the girls' dorm and try to talk to some of them. The girls' dorm was directly across the pond from theirs, and slightly down a slope so it wasn't very visible. It had been a long tradition at Torrance for the guys to dare each other to sneak over to the girls' dorm. Sebastian hung back this time. He had tagged along in previous summers, when he was younger and completely idolized the students who came to school here, and it wasn't as exciting as he'd been led to believe.

The lack of watchable TV stayed on Sebastian's mind, and as he walked past Riley's open door an idea suddenly occurred to him.

"Hey," he nodded once, leaning on the doorframe.

"What up." Riley's voice had a low, husky quality that always managed to sound sarcastic.

"Have you ever considered using your skills for the greater good?"

"Such as?"

"Hacking our satellite feed so we can get premium channels." Sebastian strode into the room.

"I thought you had a challenge for me," Riley scoffed, turning back toward the open laptop. A few clicks of the trackpad later and the satellite connection details appeared on the screen.

"So can you do it?"

"I'll need access to the dish, but yeah of course I can."

"Come on," Sebastian led Riley across campus to the main building, then up the service stairs to the rooftop access door. He had never shown anyone his hiding place, and hoped he wouldn't regret it. Somehow he didn't think he would.

"Whoa," Riley took in the view from atop the roof. His face was lit with awe beneath the black Adidas cap he always wore backwards.

"You know, if this works we will be celebrated as gods."

"Oh, definitely." Riley fiddled with some of the cables on the back of the dish while Sebastian chattered excitedly. Riley was a good listener, even when occupied with a technical task. Most of the guys he knew would interrupt with a story of their own, or constantly try to one-up each other. But not Riley. He seemed genuinely interested in Sebastian's opinions about school, movies, or whatever. When Riley was done fixing the dish, they headed back downstairs to see if it would work.

"I can't believe you've never seen *Hackers!*" Sebastian exclaimed, continuing their conversation as they walked. "You are literally a hacker."

"If I did watch it, I'd spend the entire movie just pointing out all the ridiculous inaccuracies."

"Point taken, but that can be fun too."

They returned to the dorm and made a beeline for the common room. Ben, Scott, and the rest of the guys were right where Sebastian had left them: sprawled on every available couch or chair watching a baseball game. Scott protested loudly when Sebastian grabbed the remote and turned it off while Riley examined the black box that connected the TV to the satellite dish. After a few adjustments were made and the box was reconnected to the TV, Sebastian turned it back on. When he made it past the broadcast channels and a premium channel popped up clear as day, everyone gaped.

"Riley, you're the bomb!" Sebastian exclaimed gleefully.

"You guys did this?" Ben asked him.

"Riley did, yeah." Sebastian answered proudly, turning toward Riley with a beaming smile. But Riley was all the way in the back corner by the bookcase, hunched into a chair looking uncomfortable as all eyes in the room followed Sebastian's gaze.

"But it was actually my idea," Sebastian hurriedly admitted, bringing the attention back to himself. Riley exhaled with relief as the group cheered and turned back to Sebastian, clapping him on the shoulders. Sebastian felt buoyed by all the accolades as he began giving the group a detailed rundown of how they had accomplished their mission. He kept glancing back toward the corner surreptitiously, checking to see if Riley looked pissed about being left out. He didn't want to hog all the glory for himself unless that was what Riley wanted too.

When everyone had calmed down a bit, they all crammed onto the couch to take a look at the glorious amount of channels they now had to choose from. After their initial disappointment at the fact that free satellite didn't automatically include free porn, they finally settled on an episode of *The Sopranos*. Sebastian watched from behind the couch, feeling too keyed-up to be sitting down. Then he registered movement out of the corner of his eye and saw Riley heading out the door. He wondered why Riley didn't want any of the attention they were receiving, and why he always covered up his brilliant green locks with that black Adidas hat. Without thinking, Sebastian reached out and snatched it right off of Riley's head.

"Nice hat," Sebastian said, placing it onto his own head, though it was a little too small for him. Then he noticed that Riley was hunching down even further, with arms crossed and head down. Sebastian suddenly felt bad for taking the hat and immediately handed it back. "It looks good on you."

Sebastian heard the words leave his mouth before he even registered what he was saying.

"Thanks," Riley pulled it back on as far down as it would go.

"Okay, well, later!" Sebastian rushed out the door past a bewildered-looking Riley. He hurried across campus to his house and into his room, where he closed the door and turned his stereo volume up. What had possessed him to say that? He had never told anyone that they looked good before. It just sort of popped out.

Riley was different from the rest of the guys at school. It was more than just his hacking skills or the fact that he drove a motorcycle. He was quiet and reserved when they were all together in a group, but when it was just the two of them Riley had a wry sense of humor. The neon green hair had caught his eye immediately, but Riley's enigmatic personality seemed to keep drawing him back in again.

It's normal to notice someone who's different from everyone else, Sebastian told himself. *Just because I've never noticed anyone before now doesn't mean anything...does it?*

Eight

Riley

Riley returned to their dorm room, feeling content that they had been able to help Sebastian with his mission. They couldn't remember the last time they had just hung out with someone, no pretenses or fake small talk. Sebastian was so easy to be around- it just felt effortless. They couldn't believe they were actually here, at a school for boys, making friends with other guys. Their energy couldn't be contained indoors, so Riley grabbed their helmet from the back of the closet and headed out across the grounds. It was time to take the bike out of storage.

But when Riley walked around the side of the potting shed and saw the empty space where their motorcycle had been, all happiness turned to dread. Someone had found it. They looked around frantically, thinking maybe it was hidden behind a different boulder or something, but there was no sign of it. Not knowing what else to do, they continued walking around until they reached the back of Torrance Academy and went straight toward the Dean's house.

Sebastian was sitting on his front lawn, throwing a frisbee for his pit bull terrier. The sun was setting behind the towering pines that ringed the campus, casting deep, pointed shadows across the grass. Sebastian didn't appear to notice Riley approaching; he seemed to be lost in thought. Riley almost didn't want to burden him, but they had no one else to turn to.

"Hey," Riley sat down beside him. Sebastian immediately tensed up at the sound of their voice, then shifted away from them, not meeting their eyes. The silvery-gray dog bounded over to Riley and covered their face in slobbery kisses.

"So…weird thing happened." Riley told Sebastian, wiping their face on their sleeve and soothing the dog with affectionate pats. "My bike's gone."

"What?" Sebastian's eyebrows shot up. "I told you not to leave it there."

"I'm aware of that."

"Well don't look at me," Sebastian snapped. "I didn't tell anyone about it."

"I wasn't accusing you," Riley softened their tone. Sebastian didn't seem like his usual jovial self. They had only known him for a week, but every time they interacted with him before he had been friendly and boisterous. "But what if my stepdad did come and take it after all?"

"If he came all the way up here there's no way we wouldn't have heard about it." Sebastian shook his head, then thought for a moment. "I bet it was Bob."

"Bob?"

"The groundskeeper. He's been here longer than I have. Knows the place backwards and forwards. I bet he found it."

Riley groaned and flopped backward onto the grass. The dog lay down beside them, belly up and wriggling happily. "Either way, I'll never get it back now. What the hell am I gonna do?"

"How am I supposed to know?" Sebastian was acting surly and Riley had no idea why.

"Sorry, geez." Riley jumped up and started to stalk away, cursing themself for deciding to trust him in the first place. In the short time they'd known him, Riley had come to rely on Sebastian being there with a friendly smile or some random advice. It was their mistake; they knew it had to be too good to be true. But

then they felt a strong hand grab
theirs and it stopped them short.

"Wait," Sebastian pleaded,
looking contrite. Riley held their
breath. Sebastian's hand on theirs
sent a shock of heat up and down
Riley's arm, and it was a completely
new sensation. "I'll try to help you
find it. Meet me by the common room
tonight after dinner."

"Thank you," Riley smiled with
relief, and Sebastian's mouth quirked
up in a half smile in response.
Somehow they felt like everything
would be okay now.

That night, Sebastian was
waiting at the bottom of the
staircase for Riley to join him.
Riley walked down to meet him, black
beanie completely covering their
green hair as they pulled their black
leather gloves on, tucking them into
the sleeves of their black leather
moto jacket. They immediately noticed

that Sebastian's usual smile was back in place.

"We're looking for your motorcycle, not staging a heist," he teased them. Riley shook their head and removed the gloves and jacket.

"Come on," Sebastian led them to the staff building, keys in hand. "If Bob did find it, I know where it will be. I used to sneak in here at night and borrow the ATV." He reached the door to the garage and put a key in the lock.

"Such a rebel," Riley quipped. "Didn't know I was working with a criminal."

"Takes one to know one," Sebastian returned, opening the door quietly. The large garage had an upper-level enclosed office overlooking a few vehicles stored below. Next to the office was a metal staircase, which they descended slowly, flashlights in hand.

"It's here!" Riley whispered, rushing forward. They examined their bike anxiously, making sure no harm had come to it. Sebastian stood on the other side, holding the flashlight up for them.

Suddenly a light switched on above them, overly bright in the total darkness. They both hit the deck, breathing hard in panic. But Riley saw Sebastian's face relax a moment later, and turned to see what he was looking at. The groundskeeper Bob was in his office, getting comfortable in a chair in front of his small TV. The light from the office was shining through the window into the garage. Riley exhaled, knowing that with the light on inside there was no way the groundskeeper would be able to see out through the window. They switched off their flashlights just in case.

"Shouldn't he be at home by now?" Riley asked.

Sebastian shook his head. "I forgot, it's Sunday night," he answered, as if that should explain everything.

"So he isn't off work?"

"Yeah, but he stays to watch the fights. *Sunday Night Heat*," he clarified. Riley still looked at him blankly. "Dude, now that we have satellite we can totally watch them too!" He jerked his thumb toward the office window. "His wife thinks he's at bible study." His words were muddled by barely-suppressed laughter.

"Shh!" Riley admonished him, but they were laughing along with him.

"We can sneak out quietly and he'll never know we were here."

They stood up and started rolling the bike out of the garage.

"What is that?!" A loud voice cried out from the office and they both ducked again, looking wildly toward the window. But Bob wasn't looking at them; he was still fixated on the show in front of him. "Come on, idiot, give him the chair!" he yelled at his TV.

The two dissolved into laughter, not even trying to suppress it this time. By the time they wheeled the bike out of the garage, they were both gasping for breath. Riley didn't know why Sebastian had been acting weird earlier, but was just glad that he seemed to be back to his usual upbeat self.

Nine

Riley

Riley's veins were flooded with adrenaline after successfully rescuing the motorcycle, and laughing with Sebastian felt good in a way they had never experienced before. Being around him was a rush, almost like a contact high, and they were starting to feel lightheaded.

"So, what's it like having your dad as the Dean?" Riley asked him, trying to bring themself back to Earth. As fun as this giddy feeling was, Riley didn't understand it yet.

"Well, he is *The Dean*, from the time he wakes up 'till the time he goes to sleep." Sebastian took a deep breath of the cool night air. There was no moon tonight, and the stars lit the way as he and Riley trekked across the grounds, pushing the bike by the handlebars. The campus was almost silent this time of night; only the crickets announced their presence.

"I get that." Riley was no stranger to absentee parents. "My mom might as well live on another planet, she's so out there." They laughed together again.

"Mine's in Guadalajara. She moved back home to be with Abuela after she and my dad got divorced. But she still visits a lot. She came up for my graduation in May, and I get to go see her every spring break, Thanksgiving, and alternating Christmases."

"That's cool."

"Yeah and besides, it won't be much longer, right?" Sebastian pointed out. "Soon we'll be living on our own somewhere, making our own decisions."

"Yeah, soon. I got accepted to NMTech in Socorro."

"That's awesome! I can't wait to get out of this tiny town and go to UNM in Albuquerque."

"Socorro is tiny too," Riley lamented.

"Nothing's as tiny as Glorieta."

"True, Albuquerque will probably feel like New York compared to this. So, why biology?"

"I want to go to vet school after I get my bachelor's." Sebastian led them to a part of the campus Riley had never been to before. The first thing they noticed was the smell: it was a potent mixture of sawdust, hay, and manure. Six large horses turned to look at them as they approached, ears pricked forward and tails swishing. Riley hesitated. They had never been around animals this big before.

"Check this out," Sebastian pulled one of the barn doors open and flipped on the lights. The horses all hurried in from the other side of the barn at the sound, nickering and stamping their feet impatiently. "Chill out guys, you already had dinner," Sebastian told them affectionately. He rubbed each of their foreheads in turn, and they clamored against the fence for more of his attention.

"It's okay, Riley." He beckoned them. "Come in."

Riley entered the big building cautiously. Inside, the barn was divided in half by a sturdy metal fence. The horses were all on the other side of it, and could exit to their outdoor pen through the open back doors of the barn at will. They looked even bigger up close, and Riley kept their distance. On this side of the fence, bales of hay were stacked in one corner almost up to the ceiling. In the other corner was a collection of well-used farm tools and a very old tractor covered in a thick layer of dust.

"Look, there's plenty of room right here," Sebastian indicated the space behind the old tractor. It did look big enough, but Riley still wasn't sure about this.

"Won't someone just find it again? Bob, or whoever the barn guy is?"

"It's me, Riley," Sebastian chuckled. "I'm the barn guy. I've been working here since I was twelve."

"You take care of all of them?" Riley gaped, watching the huge animals wander away from the fence now that they realized Sebastian wasn't here to feed them.

"Best job in the world," Sebastian nodded. "Just do me a favor, please?"

"Anything," Riley promised.
"You risked your neck for me tonight.
I know your dad would be beyond
pissed if he found out about this."

"Yeah, no kidding."

"So what's the favor?"

"The other guys don't know that
I work here." Sebastian rubbed a hand
on the back of his neck as he stared
down at the ground. Riley had never
seen him look so unsure of himself.
"It's hard enough being the Dean's
kid; I don't want to be treated like
the hired help on top of that."

"Of course, I won't say a
word." Riley swore to him. "And
you're sure the bike will be safe
here?"

"Positive." Sebastian answered
in that assured way he had about him.
Riley hauled the bike forward, and
Sebastian helped them push it behind
the tractor and cover it with an
extra tarp. They walked around all

sides and sure enough, none of it was visible.

"This just might work," Riley nodded in satisfaction.

"I can't believe we actually pulled this off!" Sebastian exclaimed, sitting down on a bale of hay and looking really pleased with himself. His cheeks dimpled in the most adorable way.

"Me either!" Riley joined him on the bale. The sweet smell of the hay mingled with that of the pine sawdust and the nearby horses, creating an atmosphere that was not entirely unpleasant.

"It was so...*Mission: Impossible*."

"Are you saying I look like Tom Cruise?"

"Definitely not!" Sebastian shook his head emphatically. "Tom could never pull off green hair."

"Good point," Riley snorted, then they looked at Sebastian

seriously. "Thank you, for
everything. I couldn't have done this
without you."

"You'd do the same for me."
Sebastian shrugged it off. "That's
what friends are for, right?"

"Friends," Riley murmured,
pondering the word. They hadn't had
many friends growing up, so they
weren't sure if what they were
feeling in this moment was true
friendship, or gratitude for
Sebastian's help, or something else
entirely outside of the realm of
Riley's experience. They were getting
lost in the depths of Sebastian's
eyes. Those deep brown pools pulled
them in like gravity; a force so
strong they couldn't fight it even if
they wanted to.

Before they knew what they were
doing, Riley was leaning forward
toward him until their faces were
only a breath apart. They were close
enough to feel the heat radiating off

of his skin and see the dark stubble edging the line of his jaw. Their gaze followed it down until they found themself staring at his full lips.

"Oh!" Riley exclaimed, jumping up from the hay bale as soon as they realized how close they were. "I, um, I should be getting back." They cleared their throat nervously, searching Sebastian's face to gauge his reaction.

Sebastian sat frozen in place, lips parted in surprise and a hint of a blush rising beneath the dark skin of his cheeks. What had almost just happened? Fear and uncertainty took over as they mumbled one last "thanks again". Riley turned and ran for it, spurred faster by the tumult of emotions whirling around inside them.

Ten

Sebastian

Sebastian stayed in the barn staring into space for a long time before he managed to force his feet to move. His mind was a vortex of conflict, and he was way too agitated to head home. He circled the main building before climbing the stairs to his favorite spot on the roof. What had just happened? One minute, he and Riley were having fun sneaking the motorcycle out to the barn, and the next...had Riley almost *kissed* him?

Did he *want* Riley to kiss him? Hanging around Riley felt good, in a way that none of his other friendships ever had. But did that mean it was something more? He noticed it yesterday, after their success with the satellite. He had felt happy, almost buoyant, just bringing Riley up to the roof with him and talking. And then, when he had snatched Riley's hat and worn it and it had smelled like shampoo and cologne and *Riley*...it was just too much. He needed some distance, some perspective.

The next morning, he decided he needed to avoid Riley for a while. It was impossible to think clearly when they were together, although he should have known it was going to be impossible. When he held polo practice in the arena next to the barn, Riley was there keeping time. He thought he saw Riley's eyes watching him every time he rode past, but it must have just been a trick of the sunlight. When he went to class, Riley was there hanging in the back like always. If he happened to glance behind him, Riley's head was always just turning away from him. But even outside of their times of forced proximity, the truth was that Sebastian just wasn't strong enough to stay away. He often found himself going down that same hallway toward Riley's dorm. But every time he casually walked past Riley's door, it was closed. Was Riley avoiding him too?

When it became too hot in the afternoon to stay up on the roof alone with his thoughts, Sebastian headed down the service stairs to the gymnasium. As he was passing the empty locker room, he thought he heard someone inside...singing?

Riley stood in front of the mirror, turning this way and that as if trying to decide if he looked okay. Sebastian just regarded him for a moment, and sure enough he felt that pull towards Riley as if he were a magnet and Sebastian a piece of scrap metal. He felt out of control, and that scared him. He cleared his throat loudly, and Riley whirled around, startled.

"Sebastian!" Riley's voice sounded too loud in the small space. His hand reached up to his green hair, tucking it behind an ear while looking down at his feet. Sebastian had noticed this habit of his before, and wondered why Riley always tried to hide his face. He wanted to move that hand out of the way so he could see Riley's eyes, but decided to keep some distance between them instead.

"Hey." Sebastian steeled himself for what he had to say next. "I just...wanted to...clear some things up? About the other day. I think...maybe we should take a beat. You know, some space might be good for both of us." The words came out in a jumble. He was mucking this up horribly, and Riley looked at him with an unfathomable expression.

"Okay. I was just about to go for a ride, so, guess I'll see you later." Riley picked up the keys and helmet that were housed in a nearby locker and moved to walk past him out the door. Sebastian didn't know what he had expected, but it wasn't this. He had said what he felt needed to be said, but he didn't want things to end this way either. He held his hand out to Riley before he could leave.

"Still friends?" he asked, equally terrified of either answer.

Riley took his hand and shook it, finally looking him in the eyes. Sebastian felt his resolve melt under the weight of that gaze, and he kept Riley's hand in his for much longer than he intended. It fit perfectly inside his own, warm and soft. Electric energy surged up his arm from where their skin met.

"Still friends," Riley agreed, and instant relief washed through him. "Let me know when- *if*- you want to hang out again." Riley's voice broke on the last word, or maybe it was just Sebastian's imagination.

"I will." Sebastian realized he was still holding Riley's hand and released it quickly, smoothing his hair back nervously. Riley headed off down the hallway, leaving Sebastian to shut the door. He felt a deep ache as he watched Riley disappear around the corner, and suddenly had a sinking feeling that he had just ruined the best thing he'd ever had.

Sebastian wandered slowly in the opposite direction, hands shoved into his jean pockets, shoulders hunched as one thought screamed loudly in his head.

Oh my god, I think I'm gay.

Eleven

Riley

Riley felt unmoored without
Sebastian by their side every day.
How had they managed to get so used
to his presence in such a short time?
They knew he was avoiding them
because they almost kissed him in the
barn, and found their thoughts
constantly wandering back to that
moment. What would have happened if
they *had* kissed him? Judging by his
sudden need for space, Riley imagined
it would have been a complete
disaster. And yet they couldn't seem
to stop thinking about what it might
have felt like…

"Fate!" Lincoln exclaimed,
startling Riley out of their reverie.
"What does it mean? Does it even
exist?"

"I don't think it does." one of the guys answered.

"Why not?"

"Because if we're not in control of our own lives, what's the point of anything?"

"Exactly!" Lincoln responded. "What, indeed, is the point? Read "The Appointment in Samarra" and have your essay to turn in by the end of the week. Let me know what *you* think the point is."

Riley pondered this conundrum for quite a while. They tended to agree that the idea of fate seemed bogus, but after recent events they weren't sure about anything at all. If fate was real, why would they be sent here to meet Sebastian, only to be rejected by the first person they had ever felt interested in?

To compensate for the sudden void in their life, Riley threw themself into their physical fitness regime. They were tired of straggling

behind the group during every
exercise, so they spent most of their
spare time out on the obstacle course
in the pond. While the exertion was
an excellent outlet for their
restless energy, unfortunately it
left plenty of room for their mind to
drift. And it drifted back to
Sebastian almost every time.

They watched with amazement as
he galloped past them on horseback,
coaching both teams of three players
from the sidelines, suddenly thankful
that they had decided to sign up for
the polo club. They sat behind him in
class, surreptitiously studying the
way the muscles of his neck connected
to the tops of his shoulders or the
way his cheeks dimpled when he
smiled. But whenever it seemed like
he was about to look in their
direction, debilitating fear took
hold and forced them to look away.
Riley was certain that he would never
speak to them again.

By the end of the second week of school, Riley's extra practice sessions were beginning to pay off. They were running fast enough now to catch pieces of the conversation between the two guys in front of them, who both looked like they were barely jogging just to keep up appearances.

"What are you even gonna say to her?" one of them, a guy with spiky blond hair, asked the other.

"I haven't figured that out yet," the other guy frowned. "I thought we could go over there again this weekend and use their court, maybe she'll be outside like last time."

"And then what, hope she just, like, spontaneously realizes you're the one she's been waiting for?"

Riley snorted at that, and both guys turned around to look at them in surprise.

"What's up…O'Reilly?" the dark-haired guy asked.

"O'Brien actually. Riley O'Brien."

"Whatever, I was close. So you think something's funny?"

"No," Riley hurried to cover for themself. "No, it's just…not that big a deal."

"What's not?"

"Talking to girls." They both gaped at Riley like there were lobsters crawling out of their ears. "I mean, girls are just people, right?"

"He's full of it." Blond spikes scoffed. "I bet he's never talked to a girl in his life."

If they only knew how many conversations I've had with girls. Riley thought sardonically. It had always baffled them how weird the girls in high school had acted whenever guys came around. Apparently the guys weren't any different. It seemed like Riley was the only one who was different. Again.

"Hold up, let him speak." Dark-haired guy was looking intently at Riley now, and they had to fight the urge to squirm. They hated feeling scrutinized, but the way they had both referred to them as "he" had sent a strange thrill through them. They weren't ready to lose that feeling yet.

"I'm just saying, talk to her like a person. Like how we're talking right now."

"Yeah, right. That would never work."

"Seriously, man, there's no way it's that easy."

"Fine then, go ahead with your plan to- what was it? Play basketball in front of her?" Riley moved to walk past them when they were stopped by a hand on their shoulder.

"You talk a big game, bro. You think it's so easy, how bout you prove it?"

"Uh, what?"

"Yeah, show us how it's done. Let's go over to the girls' dorm right now."

"Right now?"

"Look, if you can't do it-"

"Whatever, let's just go." Riley rolled their eyes and trudged forward toward the other side of the pond. Apparently, not having anyone to talk to all week had made them desperate.

The three of them made their way around to the girls dorm faster than expected. Riley still hadn't come up with a plan for how to approach one of the girls. Everything they said had been true, they didn't find it any more challenging talking to a girl than to anyone else. It was just the prospect of walking up to someone- anyone- that they don't know

and starting a conversation that
still seemed impossible.

They were spared from having to
prove their point when they reached
the front of the dorms and saw that
another guy was already there talking
to not one but two of the girls. His
back was to them, but his posture was
relaxed as he laughed and joked with
them. He made it look just as easy as
Riley had promised. The girl with the
blond ponytail had her hand on his
shoulder, and the red-head was
smiling at him.

Riley was relieved to not have
to follow through on their boasting,
and they wondered who it was that had
saved them from making a fool of
themself. But just as they got
closer, the guy who was flirting with
the girls turned his head, and Riley
was hit with a jolt of recognition
that sent their heart straight down
into their stomach.

It was Sebastian.

Twelve

Sebastian

Sebastian had been trying all week to sort out his feelings about Riley, but he was no closer to figuring it out now than he was at that moment in the barn. His thoughts constantly returned to wondering what would have happened if Riley had kissed him. What would it have felt like?

He needed someone to talk to. He almost blurted it out to Ben during their one-on-one game, but stopped himself just in time. Then the solution came to him all of a sudden, and he couldn't believe he hadn't thought of it sooner.

The bright June sunlight glinted off of the pond as Sebastian quickly made his way around it to reach Torrance Girls' dormitory. It was a mirror image of the boys' dorm, a two-story brick building with tall windows and ornate furnishings. He was about to pull on the heavy wooden front door when it was pushed open from the inside, and he almost crashed right into the person he was looking for.

Ella Waterson was one of the rare Torrance students who also lived in Glorieta. She had signed up for every one of his father's college-prep seminars all throughout high school, and since Sebastian was required to attend as well they had ended up spending each summer together for the past four years.

"'Basti!" She sounded so happy to see him, he didn't even cringe at the use of his childhood nickname while he gave her a one-armed hug in greeting.

"Hey El, how's school?"

"Oh, you know, pretty intense."

"I'm sure you're killing it," he reassured her. Sebastian knew she had gotten into Torrance Girls' on one of the few scholarships offered by the Academy, and as a result she seemed to feel like she always had to work twice as hard to prove that she belonged here.

"How about you?"

"Honestly..." he hesitated briefly, but then realized that if he could talk to anyone about his situation it would be Ella. "It's not at all what I thought it would be like."

"'Oft expectation fails, and most oft there where most it promises.'"

"Okay, brainiac, translate please?"

"I just meant that- oof!" The giant door was once again pushed open from the inside, and unfortunately Ella was still standing right in front of it. It bumped her shoulder, and she reached forward to grasp Sebastian's arm as she lost her balance.

"Omigod, Ella, could you be more in the way?" the girl coming through the doorway complained.

"Sebastian, this is my roommate Kate."

"*This* is your little summer-school study buddy?" Kate appraised him with raised eyebrows. "I was expecting Screech, but he's *much* more of a Zack. No wonder you've been keeping him all to yourself. Please tell me he has a friend for me?" Sebastian laughed aloud at her comparison. He'd always thought of himself as a Slater, personally.

"I told you it's not like that," Ella scowled at her. Sebastian's smile faded, and he was about to lend his support to Ella's defense when Kate spoke again.

"Oh wow, ask and you shall receive."

Sebastian whirled around to see what she was talking about, and his heart leapt into his throat when he saw Riley striding toward him with Ben and Scott. They were all wearing their gym clothes and looked like they had just finished running laps. Everyone stood in silence for a second that seemed to stretch on for too long while Sebastian filled his eyes with the sight of the person he'd been thinking about all week long.

"Um, hey." Riley broke the awkward silence. Sebastian snapped himself out of his momentary brain freeze.

"Hi there," Kate was beaming at the new arrivals, and Ella's cheeks had suddenly turned a bright crimson.

"Riley, Ben, Scott, this is my friend Ella and her roommate-"

"Kate," she interrupted him to step forward and offer her hand to Riley. "You know, you look *so* much like my ex-boyfriend."

"Oh, uh, sorry..." Riley stammered.

"It's a compliment, don't worry. He was an ass, but a very hot ass. We were just talking about going to the movie on the lawn tonight. Maybe you all can meet us there?"

"Sounds cool, we'll be there." Scott answered before Sebastian could think of an excuse. Ben nodded, but didn't say anything.

Ella was looking everywhere except at the guys. Kate's gaze focused back on Riley, clearly appreciating what she saw and not trying to hide it.

"See you tonight, Riley."

Thirteen

Riley

As soon as the girls were out of earshot, Ben and Scott erupted into uproarious praise of Riley's apparent superpower of being able to talk to girls.

"Dude, how did you do that?" Ben clapped them on the shoulder.

"Seriously, that hot chick was so into you!" Scott added. Sebastian was notably silent as the four of them walked back across the grass toward their dorms. Riley didn't see what the big deal was, they'd barely said two words to her. How that was deserving of any accolades was beyond them.

Riley spent a long time getting ready for movie night. They tried on every outfit before deciding on a blue button-up and jeans. They couldn't help but feel like this was a date; just not the date they wanted to be on. They had never been so blatantly hit-on by a girl before, and couldn't decide if it felt weird or flattering. Sebastian, on the other hand, had definitely been weird. He had been talking and laughing with the girls, but as soon as Riley joined him he had clammed right up.

Riley had done what Sebastian asked and given him space. It was killing them to have to stay away from him, but if that's what he needed then so be it. He kept glancing up in Riley's general direction whenever they had to be in close proximity for school, but every time it happened he would look away quickly, not giving Riley enough time to read the emotions in his eyes. They were dying to ask him if he had been thinking about them, about their almost-kiss and what it meant. They were also terrified of the answer.

Finally, after their hair looked adequately styled, Riley looked for Sebastian and the guys out on the lawn by the pond. They half-expected Sebastian to just not show up, leaving Riley to fend for themself with Kate all evening. But there he was standing next to her and Ella on the grass, looking fresh-faced if a little tense. Riley couldn't help but remember that first day, when Sebastian had approached them and offered to help with hiding their motorcycle. It seemed like so long ago, but in reality it had only been a few weeks.

"O'Brien!" Ben called out as he and Scott joined them. Together they walked over toward Sebastian, Ella, and Kate. When she spotted Riley her entire face brightened and she waved them over. Sebastian unfurled a blanket and laid it out on the ground for the six of them. He sat down next to Ella, and Kate got comfortable in between him and Riley. Kate was wearing a sundress that showed off a lot of her suntanned skin, and her red curls brushed the tops of her bare shoulders as she turned her head to speak to them. But Riley wasn't listening to her; they were looking over her head at Sebastian and Ella.

They were clearly at ease with each other, talking in low voices and laughing frequently. Ella was leaning back on her elbows, long blonde hair cascading down to the blanket beneath her. Seeing the two of them together sent a strong pain through Riley's heart. *Was this the type of person he wanted to be dating? Maybe they already are!* Riley suddenly realized with a lump in their throat that they had no idea if Sebastian was already with someone. He had never mentioned it, but Riley had never asked either.

Then Ella abruptly stopped laughing when Ben sat down on the other side of her. She sat up straight, crossing her legs and picking at the grass in front of her. Riley wondered if she was upset that he had interrupted her conversation with Sebastian. Scott wedged himself in between Sebastian and Kate, causing her to scoot even closer to Riley. They tried to subtly shift as close to the edge of the blanket as possible. It wasn't far enough, because Kate's manicured pinky finger was now grazing the side of their hand. Riley could already feel the hysterics building up inside them at the impossible situation they were in. All they could do was keep their mouth clamped shut and hope to god they didn't start laughing uncontrollably. They should never have agreed to this, but the prospect of spending time with Sebastian had been too good to pass up.

Romeo + Juliet cued up on the giant temporary screen in front of them, and Riley settled in for a long evening of awkwardness.

"This movie's so romantic," Kate leaned over and whispered in Riley's ear.

"What? You know they both die at the end, right?"

"At least they got to feel that all-encompassing love before they died."

"I'd risk exile and death for Claire Danes," Scott added.

"You have to admit, the way they make Shakespeare actually sound cool is pretty dope," Sebastian was looking at Riley as he spoke, and hope welled up inside them. It was the most he had said to them in ages.

"I guess the soundtrack's okay, so at least there's that." Riley acknowledged, though a smile threatened at the corner of their lips.

"You guys are completely missing the point," Kate grumbled, obviously disappointed that they weren't paying attention to her anymore.

"Riley doesn't watch a lot of movies," Sebastian smiled at them, and Riley could have floated right up to the stars in that moment.

"Well, I can fix that," Kate slid her hand a little farther to place it on top of Riley's. They immediately pulled away from her, then stood up to cover their reaction.

"I'm gonna go get some popcorn," Riley told the group and left hurriedly, wondering why they had agreed to come along at all.

Fourteen

Sebastian

Sebastian felt like the air had been forced out of his lungs the second Riley left. He had almost forgotten how good it felt to be around him, how his smile alone could make him feel like he was the only person in the room. The truth was, he had been trying to forget, but it wasn't working, not really. He could distract himself as much as possible but at the end of the day his thoughts always returned to Riley. All he wanted now was for everyone else to go away so he could sit with Riley alone, laughing and joking like they used to.

But there was Kate, and as soon as Riley was out of earshot she pounced.

"Finally!" she squeezed herself in between him and Ella.

"Finally what?"

"Tell me everything you know about Riley! Do you think he likes me?"

Sebastian frowned.

"I thought we had a moment," Kate continued. "But maybe that's just my wishful thinking. He's so hard to read."

Tell me about it, Sebastian thought, but only nodded. Kate was still talking.

"But that's actually what I like about him."

"Yeah, me too." Sebastian found himself agreeing out loud. Kate didn't seem to hear him.

"He's not like other guys, he's more..."

"Mysterious?" Ella supplied.

"Exactly! Would you please talk to him for me, Sebastian?"

"No!" Sebastian practically shouted. "I mean, it would be weird."

"What would be weird, you talking to him or us getting together?"

"Both?" Sebastian hedged. "I don't know for sure, but I don't think you're Riley's type."

"Really." Kate pursed her lips and appraised him anew. Sebastian shrank down on the blanket, wondering if he had revealed too much but not quite able to bring himself to care if he had. After a moment she scooted closer to Ella and the two girls continued their conversation in whispers punctuated by giggles. Sebastian glanced over at Ben on the other side of Ella, but he just shrugged.

Riley didn't return for the rest of the movie. That didn't surprise him, but he was completely blindsided as he was leaving to see that Riley was still hanging out near the concessions. He started to walk over, but Kate got there first. Sebastian watched with dismay as she blatantly flirted with Riley, but when she leaned in closer he couldn't take it anymore. He turned away from the scene and rushed home without a backward glance.

Fifteen

Riley

As Riley watched Sebastian walking away, they felt like the sun was setting and darkness was closing in. They had listened when Sebastian told them that he wanted distance from them, which Riley interpreted to mean that he didn't like them in *that* way- the way that meant almost sneaking a kiss after a motorcycle heist. But they had maintained hope, however futilely, that maybe he would change his mind. So they had lingered around the popcorn cart waiting for the movie to end in case he might come talk to them.

Instead, it was Kate who showed up.

"Hey Riley,"

"Oh, hey." They nodded once in her direction but kept looking over her shoulder for Sebastian.

"So…I just wanted to tell you that tonight was really fun." Her face was open and hopeful.

"Um…yeah, it was."

"And I was thinking…I mean I was wondering if maybe next movie night it could be just the two of us?"

"Kate I..." Riley had no idea how to handle this situation. They didn't want to hurt her feelings, but they already knew there was no way that they could reciprocate.

"I think you're really cool," Kate went on, stepping even closer to Riley.

"I think you're cool, too." Riley backed up until they were practically sitting in the popcorn machine.

"If you don't want to see a movie, that's totally fine. I was just hoping we could hang out again or...something." Kate put a hand on Riley's shoulder. Her face was inches from theirs now, filling their entire field of vision.

"Wait!" Riley cried out to stop her from actually kissing them. "Kate, this isn't going to work."

Kate's face went beet red and her eyes filled with tears. She turned to leave, but Riley stopped her so they could explain.

"No, hold on, don't leave." Riley took her hands and looked into her blue eyes, willing her to understand. "We can definitely hang out as friends, but the truth is… I kinda like someone else."

"Sebastian was right," Kate closed her eyes and sighed. "This was a bad idea."

"You talked to Sebastian about me?"

"I'm sorry if I crossed a line, I just really needed advice about how

to approach you. He told me he didn't
see you and me working out. I guess
he knows you pretty well."

Riley's mind began whirling
with this information. Had Sebastian
said that because he really didn't
think Riley and Kate would work out
together, or because he thought Riley
would work better with someone else?
Someone like him? The kernel of hope
expanded inside them. Riley searched
the crowd once more, and that was
when they spotted Sebastian walking
away from them at a fast pace. Their
heart sank. Nothing had changed.

"It's okay," they patted Kate's
arm awkwardly, not wanting to hurt
her feelings even more but needing to
end this conversation. They were
doing their best to hold it together
until she left and they could wallow
in peace.

Later that night Riley tossed
and turned, reliving all the events
of the evening in their mind. They

replayed the moment when Kate tried to kiss them, and how uncomfortable it made them feel. Then a horrible thought struck home: *was that how Sebastian had felt when Riley almost kissed him?*

Sixteen

Sebastian

Sebastian spent the rest of the weekend agonizing over whether or not Kate made a move on Riley, and whether or not Riley reciprocated. It didn't help that everyone at practice was buzzing about how Riley totally scored with the hot chick from California. His guts were so twisted up inside him he could barely eat. His dad thought he must have a stomach bug and made him stay in bed on Sunday. Finally it was all too much, he just had to find out for himself. He was heading toward the dorms when he saw Riley walking across campus alone and rushed to catch up.

"Hey!"

"Hey," Riley turned around and smiled at him in a way that was so disarming he felt like he was tumbling forward into an infinite abyss. Then Riley's smile faded, replaced by a very guarded expression. Sebastian faltered. Had he already done something to mess things up again?

"Okay, look," he started, thinking he was ready to spill his guts but then immediately chickening out. "I want you two to be happy together." It was true, he really did want Riley to be happy. Even if that meant being with someone other than him.

"You want who to be happy?"

"You and Kate." He braced himself for what was sure to be the painful confirmation of what he'd been fearing.

There was a moment of shocked silence, and then Riley burst into laughter.

Sebastian blinked in surprise. Riley never reacted the way he expected. That was part of the appeal, but it also kept him off balance.

"Didn't she tell you after the movie on Friday?" he asked, too nervous to laugh along. "She likes you." He studied Riley's face, trying to ascertain his true feelings about the situation, but he was as inscrutable as ever. "Not that I really care." Sebastian deflected at the last minute.

Riley stopped laughing, lips pressing together in a frown. Sebastian wasn't fooling anyone.

"You want me to be happy, but you don't really care?" Riley repeated slowly, and Sebastian cringed. When he heard it that way it sounded ridiculous.

"I don't know what you want me to say." Sebastian sighed heavily.

"How about you start with what you really think?"

"Well, do you like her?"

"Oh yeah, in the five words we exchanged with each other we really hit it off."

"Look, whatever happens I'm...I'm cool with it." He could barely get the words out, but he didn't want to stand in the way if this is what Riley wanted. "She likes you, so you should go for it."

"And that's what you *really* think?" Riley looked up at him, green eyes flecked with amber searching his face for the truth behind his words.

"Yes." Sebastian turned and walked quickly away before Riley could see the pain in his eyes.

Seventeen

Riley

It wasn't just Sebastian who seemed convinced that Riley and Kate were now a thing. Every time they left their room, Riley was bombarded with questions about her.

"Hey, O'B!" Ben called loudly from the common room as Riley passed.

"O-B-1," Scott added with a mock Jedi bow.

"Cut it out, guys, I'm not Obi Wan."

"Anyone who can land a chick like Kate in one night is the master."

"Ugh, I did not 'land' anyone, okay?"

"Dude, don't be stingy! Tell us how you do it."

"I didn't do anything. You were there too."

"Yeah, I was sitting right next to her and she was all over you, man. What's your secret?"

"Honestly, I wish I knew." Riley sighed, then continued walking. Apparently the exchange of a few words followed by an almost-kiss constituted dating in this universe. But if that were true, why couldn't things be that simple with Sebastian?

On Monday, Lincoln was holding class out on the lawn reading a poem by Browning. Robert, of course, not Elizabeth Barrett. Riley was planning to tune it all out like they usually did, but today it was Sebastian's turn to read aloud. Riley had been keeping as much distance between themself and Sebastian as possible, even more than when he had asked them for space. They were even okay letting him think they might be interested in Kate. Anything was better than confronting the very real possibility that Sebastian had been repulsed when Riley had almost kissed him. But hearing Sebastian's voice breathing life into the poem, Riley became entranced. There was no harm in just listening to him, was there?

The poem was about deciding that society in all its complexities is overrated, and at the end of the day all a person needs is to come home to their quiet life with the person they love. Riley had never even entertained the possibility of falling for a guy when they were scheming to enroll in an all-boys academy. The goal here was to be able to be themself, that was it.

Riley had known they were different all their life. They screamed bloody murder every time their mom tried to make them wear a dress, and would steal scissors to chop off their own hair if they weren't taken to a barber to have it done. Riley knew without having to be told that most people born female didn't feel this strongly about things like that.

And then their stepdad, on the rare occasions that he noticed them at all, started with the name-calling. Words like 'butch' and 'dyke'. Even as a young person Riley knew what those words meant: a girl who liked to kiss other girls. But Riley had never kissed a girl, had never even come close to kissing anyone until...Sebastian. With his deep brown eyes that expressed his every thought.

Sebastian hadn't looked horrified when they leaned in close to him that day in the barn. He hadn't jumped backward or protested loudly like Riley had with Kate. But that didn't mean he had wanted them to kiss him. Riley felt horrible that they might have made him uncomfortable, and resolved to keep their distance for good this time. No more impromptu movie nights.

Riley was so lost in their contemplation that they didn't realize Lincoln had called on them until the rest of the class started laughing.

"Riley?" Lincoln repeated. "Any thoughts you'd like to share with the class?"

Riley's eyes immediately went to Sebastian, but then quickly looked away hoping no one had noticed.

"Uh, not really."

"Guys, poetry is about expressing your deepest emotions," Lincoln implored them. "If you keep everything bottled in you'll eventually explode, and I don't want to be in charge of cleaning up that mess."

Everyone laughed again.

"I'm serious, you have to find an outlet for this stuff. Trust me on this." Lincoln looked at each of them in turn. "Okay, your assignment this week is to pick a song that fully resonates with your soul. Bring in a CD on Friday, and we'll all listen and talk more about this. Until then, back to the classics." He dismissed them, and Riley uncrossed their legs to stand up. They already knew what song they would pick. They had been listening to it on repeat all weekend, and it suddenly occurred to them that this might be a perfect opportunity. When they play this song in class on Friday, Sebastian will have to listen to it and then he will know how they really feel about him.

As soon as Riley got back to their room, they played their favorite song again and spent the rest of the afternoon contemplating the inevitability of falling for someone who might never feel the same way about them.

Eighteen

Sebastian

Friday morning during polo practice, Sebastian listened to Riley's voice calling out start and stop times through the loudspeaker. It was the closest contact they had these days, and he relished it. Riley sat on the announcer's platform overlooking the team of riders as they executed training drills on horseback. During these sessions, Sebastian allowed his gaze to drift up to where Riley sat every time he passed by. With his helmet shading the top half of his face, no one - including Riley - would ever be the wiser.

When training ended and the horses were cooled off and brushed down, Sebastian instructed them all to clean the saddles and bridles. Most of the guys spent the time razzing each other about who they wanted to invite to the upcoming Fourth of July Formal. Sebastian was joking around with them while carrying out a bunch of tack to be cleaned.

"So Ben, when are you gonna ask Ella out?" Sebastian teased his friend, and when Ben moved to shove him he dodged nimbly. As he spun out of reach, he felt the stirrups smack into something solid. Someone cried out, and Sebastian dropped the saddle and whirled back around. He knew that voice.

"Crap, I'm so sorry! Are you okay?" he asked Riley.

"Yeah, I'm tougher than I look." Riley laughed it off. "But are you two done horsing around? I just want to make sure I stay out of the danger zone."

Sebastian snorted at Riley's horse pun, though none of the other guys laughed.

"Yeah, I'm pretty sure Ben is too chicken, anyway." Sebastian jibed. Riley backed away quickly, heading toward the barn.

"Too chicken to take you down? Please!" Ben grabbed Sebastian in a headlock.

"I meant too chicken to ask Ella out!" Sebastian mumbled from underneath Ben's arm. Ben kicked his legs out from under him and they both collapsed onto the grass, laughing.

"Two-time state wrestling champ, bro." Ben reminded him. "Don't mess with me."

"Understood," Sebastian huffed, trying to catch his breath. "But seriously man, you've been into her ever since term started. Why not give it a shot?"

"If it's so easy, who are you asking?" Ben countered, and Sebastian felt his face get burning hot. He was reminded for what felt like the hundredth time that he couldn't ask the one person he would actually want to go with.

"I'm going with Kate," he lied, and instantly regretted it. Not only was she the last person he would ask, but she was surely already going with Riley.

"You asked Kate? As in, Riley's Kate?" Ben sounded disapproving, and Sebastian felt even worse. *Riley's Kate.* He dropped his head backward onto the ground with a thump. His stomach felt unsteady, and he suddenly worried he was about to vomit. The thought of Riley dancing with Kate, arms around each other while she looked at him with that sickening, adoring face...he wouldn't be able to stand it.

"Okay fine, you got me!" he admitted with a groan. "I haven't asked anyone yet."

"You're such a hypocrite!" Ben smacked him half-heartedly on the shoulder. "We could always just go solo, see who we meet up with when we get there."

"No, that's lame." Sebastian shook his head. He definitely didn't want to show up dateless to watch Riley having a great time with Kate. "How about this: I'll ask Ella out for you, and you find someone for me to go with?"

"You would do that for me?"

"Yeah, of course. What are friends for?"

"Alright, deal." Ben held out his hand and they shook on it.

That afternoon Sebastian still didn't have a song to bring to class. How was he supposed to pick one song that represented everything he was feeling inside? He hated getting an incomplete, but couldn't think of what else to do. Class met in the music room today, which was stocked with a fairly decent sound system. Everyone was gathered around it, talking excitedly about their favorite bands and concerts they had been to. Just another reminder of things Sebastian had missed out on. The Dean was always too busy to take him to shows, or to do much of anything at all with him other than homeschooling.

Lincoln arrived and called the class to order. He asked if everyone had brought their CDs, and Sebastian hunched in the back of the group trying to make himself invisible. Riley, on the other hand, volunteered to share first. Lincoln placed the CD into the stereo and selected Riley's track. "Everything You Want" by Vertical Horizon came blasting out of the speakers, and the lyrics hit Sebastian right in the chest. He felt like a large balloon was inflating inside his ribs, constricting his lungs and pushing his heart up into his throat. Not knowing what else to do, he turned and fled before the song had even ended.

Sebastian ran all the way home and into his room without stopping. He closed himself inside, breath ragged as he tried to process everything he was feeling. Something about the song Riley played had gutted him. How could Riley do that? How could he play that song, while looking at him across the room like that, when he's with Kate now? Sebastian knew he had screwed everything up; he wished so much that he could go back in time and change it all. But he couldn't, and now Riley was with someone else. He felt like his heart had been ripped out and left on the floor of the music room at Riley's feet.

Sebastian dragged himself out of the house the next day. He couldn't stay in his room one minute longer; the walls were starting to feel like they were closing in on him. He needed to get out of his own head, get some perspective. He needed a friend, and he caught a ride into town with Bob so he could talk to Ella. She worked weekends at the one department store on the town's tiny main street. She greeted him with a genuine smile when she saw him walk in.

"Hey El," he returned her smile warmly.

"So good to see you, 'Basti." She replied as she folded and restocked pairs of jeans. "How've you been?"

"Not great, actually." Sebastian hesitated, wondering if Ella was close with her roommate Kate. But the more he thought about it, the more he realized that he really needed to talk to her. After all, they'd been friends for years. And Kate had only arrived for the summer. Surely that counted for something? And then he found himself unloading the entire story onto her while helping her work. Ella listened diligently, interjecting with sympathetic sounds here and there.

"Wow, it sounds like you really like Riley," Ella pointed out when he finished.

"I mean, yeah," Sebastian admitted. "Yeah, I really do." Saying it out loud was like setting down a weight he had been carrying on his shoulders for weeks. "But I have no idea what I'm supposed to do!"

"Well I don't know much either, but in my very limited experience I've learned that keeping things inside is never the right course of action."

"Ugh, you're starting to sound like Lincoln."

"Well, maybe he has a point." Ella insisted, elbowing him in the ribs as he continued rehanging the T-shirts after she tagged them.

"Speaking of which, my friend Ben wants to take you to the Fourth Formal. You interested?"

"Ben?" she squeaked, her voice suddenly rising an octave as her cheeks pinked.

"I take that as a yes?" Sebastian laughed. Ella only nodded, hiding her face behind more shirts. "I'll let him know." Sebastian was glad that at least one of them would get to go with the person that they

wanted to.

Nineteen

Riley

Riley had watched with dismay as Sebastian rushed out of the music room during their song. They had thought this would be the perfect way to get through to him, to let him know how they really feel about him without putting either of them on the spot. But it seemed like everything they did was too much, and every time they tried to get closer to him they just ended up pushing him farther away.

Saturday morning Riley finished another run around the pond. Their time was improving, but still the slowest in the class. On their way toward the gym to shower, they passed Ben and Scott. They tried to scoot around them inconspicuously to avoid more questions about Kate, but they couldn't help lingering when they heard Sebastian's name.

"Sebastian's really going to ask Ella?" Scott sounded skeptical.

"That's what he said, but I'll believe it when I see it," Ben agreed.

"What do you think she would say if he does?"

"If she says yes I'll eat my left foot."

Riley felt sick. Sebastian was going to ask Ella to the dance? It was obvious at the movie that the two of them were close, and Riley had wondered if they might be together. But Sebastian had never mentioned her, not once. They felt like a world-class idiot. Here they were agonizing over a song, while Sebastian was already taken. They tried to hurry away, but of course they tripped over their own feet and went sprawling across the lawn in plain sight of Scott and Ben.

"Look, it's O-B-1!"

"You alright, O'Brien?" Ben helped them up.

"I'm fine."

"Where's your girlfriend?" Scott wondered.

"For the last time, Kate's not my girlfriend."

"So that means she's available? Maybe I'll ask her out then."

"Don't even think about it, I call dibs." Ben elbowed his friend, and Riley took advantage of the distraction to make their exit. They were starting to think they would never understand other people.

Adding insult to injury, on their way back out of the main building after showering they ran into Kate and Ella of all people.

"Oh, hey guys." Riley scrutinized Ella in the sunlight: her blonde ponytail bobbed as she walked, her cheeks rosy as she smiled at them in a completely guileless way. It was going to be really hard to hate her.

"Hi Riley," she beamed.

"So Ben just came to ask me about the dance," Kate brightened as they approached. "But I wanted to talk to you one more time before I give him an answer. If you're available, I'd much rather go with you."

Riley hated being put in this position. They hated having to constantly fend off inquiries about her, and then hurt her feelings not once but twice. But they couldn't go to the dance with her knowing they could never return her feelings.

"I'm sorry Kate, but I told you before, I like someone else."

"And did this 'someone else' agree to go to the dance with you?" she asked pointedly.

"Well, no, but…"

"We could go as friends then."

"No, Kate, we couldn't." Riley sighed.

"Fine. You'd rather go alone than go with me, well that's just…whatever!" Kate stormed off, leaving them alone with Ella.

"Don't worry, Riley, she'll be okay." Ella placed a comforting hand on their shoulder. "If I know anything about Kate, it's that she doesn't let anything keep her down for long."

"Good, that's good. You're a good friend." Riley babbled in an effort to keep themself from screaming the question he wanted to ask Ella. *Are you going out with Sebastian?*

"Will *you* be okay?" Ella's genuine question shook them out of their thoughts.

"Oh, I...um…don't know yet."

"Do you want to talk about it?"

"How well do you know Sebastian?" The question was out before they could stop themself.

"He's my summer-school friend." Ella smiled fondly.

"You've done the Torrance Academy 'Boot Camp' more than once?"

"Well, the pre-college immersion program is only the summer after graduation. All the previous summers we did the college-prep seminar taught by Dean Otero."

Riley whistled. "Oh dang, you guys are hard-core."

"I guess I am. But I think Sebastian was more forced into it by his dad."

"That makes sense."

"Our first summer seminar was right after his parents' divorce. He was missing his mom a lot, I'm always missing mine, and we bonded pretty much right away. So to answer your question, I'd say I know Sebastian pretty well."

"I'm glad you two had each other, at least."

"Me too."

"So were you and Sebastian ever, like, a thing?"

"Oh no, not at all," Ella assured them. "Strictly friends only."

"That's cool." Riley was flooded with relief, and they tried to rein themself back in before they got carried away. *That still doesn't mean he's not taken.* "Does he have a girlfriend or anything?"

"He's never mentioned any girls to me. Never mentioned anyone, in fact, until…"

"Until?" Riley leaned forward as their heart started to race. Ella bit her lip in uncertainty, and Riley silently pleaded with her to speak.

"Your name might have come up, once."

Riley's heart was doing full-on acrobatics now. Sebastian had

mentioned them? *Only* them? To his
summer-school friend? They took a
deep breath. They needed to calm
down. They didn't know what Sebastian
had said to her about them. He could
have just been venting about the
weirdo who tried to kiss him.

"Sebastian's a really good guy.
He wouldn't waste his energy on
someone who wasn't worth getting to
know." Ella looked them right in the
eyes, and Riley had the strong sense
that she was trying to tell them
something. They wished she'd just say
it.

"You don't know anything about
me," Riley pointed out.

"Listen, I deal with people all
day long. At school, at work. Most
people suck. I can spot the few
decent ones when they come around."

"Thank you." Riley looked down
at the ground. They weren't used to
compliments and never knew how to
respond.

"'Love sought is good, but given unsought is better.'"

"What?"

"Just talk to Sebastian, okay? Trust me." Ella patted their shoulder one last time before turning to walk back toward the girls' dorms. And Riley realized that, inexplicably, they did trust her.

Twenty

Sebastian

Sebastian dragged himself to the basketball court after school Monday afternoon. He was tired of his room; the walls were starting to feel like they were closing in on him. He got there before anyone else and started warming up until Ben arrived.

"Hey man, I thought you were sick or something," Ben told him as he joined the game. "You ran out of class on Friday looking as green as O'Brien's hair!"

Sebastian blanched at the joke. "Naw, I just needed a minute."

"Well I'm glad you're here because I actually have good news." Ben was practically bouncing on the balls of his feet. "I found you a date for this weekend and you'll never guess who it is!"

"Oh, that reminds me," Sebastian interrupted him. "Ella said yes."

"Hold up, what?" Ben's grin disappeared. "You...you actually talked to her?"

"Duh, I've been friends with her forever. Plus I told you I'd do it."

"And she said yes? To going with me?"

"Totally. I think she really likes you, man." Sebastian chuckled at the memory of Ella's red face.

"I...um...uh..." Ben stammered and Sebastian clapped him on the shoulder.

"You're welcome." He smiled at his friend.

"Guess you'd better get started." Scott told Ben as he joined them on the court.

"Started?"

"Eating your left foot!" Scott guffawed. "I can't believe she agreed to go with your sorry ass."

"At least I have a date, that's more than you can say. So does Sebastian."

"Oh yeah that's right, who is it?" Sebastian asked him.

"Hmm?"

"You said you found someone for me to go with. Who?"

"Oh, Kate." Ben's smile slowly returned. "Guess you're not such a liar after all!"

"Kate?" Sebastian screeched. "As in...*Kate?*"

"The one and only." Ben was fully grinning again. "*You're* welcome!"

"Damn, I need to get some uglier friends." Scott muttered.

Sebastian felt like bees were swarming in his ears. Everything was going hazy and nothing was making any sense. That couldn't be right. Kate was going to the dance with Riley. Kate was with Riley. That was the whole reason why Sebastian had been so miserable all week. Riley was happy. With Kate.

Suddenly Sebastian was running again, leaving Ben and Scott on the court looking mystified.

Twenty-one

Riley

Riley was staring miserably at their computer. For once their stereo was off. They couldn't bear to listen to that song anymore. They probably should just chuck it into the trash. They were out of ideas for how to reach Sebastian. Maybe it was time to just give up.

Then their door burst open and there he was, breathing hard and sweating through his sports tank.

"Sebastian?"

"You're with Kate." His voice sounded mangled.

"Excuse me?"

"You're with Kate, so why aren't you going to the Fourth of July Formal with her?"

"What are you going on about?"
Riley frowned.

"Ben asked me to ask Ella for
him, so I did and then he said he'd
find someone for me, so he did, and
that someone he found was Kate." The
words all came out of him in a rush.

"Okay, slow down." Riley stood
and moved out of the way so that
Sebastian could sit in the chair,
then they closed the door behind him
and locked it. "You're going to the
formal with Kate?"

"No!" Sebastian scrubbed his
hands down his face. Riley wanted so
much to go to him, comfort him. But
they didn't dare. They were too
afraid to push him away again. After
what felt like forever, he looked up
at them. His eyes were dark and
brimming with emotion. "I knew I
couldn't go with who I wanted to go
with so I agreed to let Ben just pick
someone for me. But he asked Kate if
she would go with me, and she said

yes which means she's not going with you. I need to know why."

"I told you before, there's nothing going on between me and Kate." Riley tried to keep their voice even, but panic was rising up inside them. Something was happening here, something they couldn't yet name.

"You never denied it," Sebastian accused.

"You never gave me the chance!"

"I saw you with her after the movie."

"I'm not interested in her that way," Riley admitted. "I told her I like someone else."

"But you…" He stopped as Riley's words caught up to him. "Someone else? Who?"

"Who did you want to go to the dance with but couldn't?" Riley countered.

They looked at each other for a long moment, realization dawning. The unspoken words hung in the air between them. Was this really happening? Was Sebastian actually telling them that *they* were the person he wanted to go to the dance with?

"So, uh," Sebastian stood from the chair, pacing the room with nervous energy. "You're definitely not going with anybody?"

"Nope." Riley fought the grin tugging at their lips as they watched Sebastian search for the right words. They didn't know how it was possible, but he was even more adorable when he was floundering and unsure of himself. "And you aren't going with anyone?"

"Definitely not."

"Then maybe we can, I don't know, meet up when we get there?" Riley held their breath, every muscle in their body tensed as they waited for his answer.

"Yeah." Sebastian nodded once, his jaw set and his eyes bright. "Okay."

"Great." Riley grinned widely now as elation filled them. "It's a date." The words were out of their mouth before they could think it through, and before the panic could take over again they went back to their door and opened it for Sebastian. He paused as he passed by them on the way out, and the weight of his gaze combined with the scent of him and his *closeness* was almost overwhelming. Riley gulped and held themself rooted to the spot, determined not to overstep again and lose whatever ground they had just regained.

"Goodnight Riley," Sebastian whispered, and then he was gone.

Twenty-two

Sebastian

"It's a date," Riley had said, and Sebastian's heart stuttered like it always did when Riley smiled at him. Riley's words echoed through him, leaving a multitude of emotions in their wake. *A date with Riley.* Excitement, dread, elation, terror. He clung to the side of the school, momentarily immobilized while he processed everything he was feeling.

It had all happened so fast, his brain hadn't fully caught up yet. The second he had found out that Riley wasn't going to the dance with Kate, he had raced over there to confront him without fully thinking it through. It was one thing to wish he could go with Riley while knowing there was no chance of it ever happening; it was quite another to consider actually doing it. But when Riley had asked him if they could meet up at the dance, he had agreed without hesitation.

Is it a date? If so, is that what he wanted? Sebastian thought about it for a second. He knew for certain that his feelings for Riley went beyond friendship. But dating? In public? What would people think? He had been dragged along to these dances as the Dean's son for years, and he had never thought twice about seeing guys hanging out in groups or pairs together. Maybe it wouldn't be a big deal.

The phone was ringing when he got back home, and Sebastian hurried to answer it.

"What are you wearing?" Riley's familiar husky voice greeted him.

"Uh..." Sebastian's mind whirled with the implications of the question and then promptly stalled out. "Didn't you just see me?"

"Not what you are wearing right now, dummy." Riley laughed. "I meant the formal."

"Oh, the dance."

"Yes."

Sebastian could picture the exact way Riley would raise both eyebrows at him.

"I'm gonna borrow my dad's tux," he answered.

"Good option," Riley agreed. "Very *Bond*."

"What about you?"

"Dunno yet. I just wanted to make sure we don't show up looking all matchy-matchy like the agents in *The Matrix*."

"I promise I'll leave my sunglasses at home," he quipped, and Riley laughed. Making Riley laugh was addictive. Most of the time he was able to elicit low chuckles that couldn't even be heard unless you were paying close attention. But the best feeling was earning one of his rare and hard-won hearty laughs. It almost felt normal again, a small glimpse of how it had felt to hang out with Riley before things got complicated. He had felt it for a moment at the movie, too, before Kate got in the way. It made him giddy, like he was full of something effervescent. If he could keep this feeling going, if he could keep himself from doing anything stupid from now on, then they might just have a chance.

And that was when Sebastian realized he already knew the answer to his question. He definitely did want this to be a date.

Twenty-three

Riley

Riley hung up the phone as a new wave of panic began setting in. They had been so thrilled at the prospect of actually going to the dance with Sebastian that they hadn't stopped to think about what in the world they were going to wear to it. They knew how to dress up as a girl. By the time they turned thirteen they were so exhausted from the constant bickering at home- over their hair and their clothes and everything else about them- that they just gave up. They willingly attended prep school with all of their mom's friends' daughters. They let their hair grow to an obscene length, falling in waves just past their shoulders. They wore makeup everyday and started signing up for every cotillion and debutante ball in existence.

Going to those events with their mom was the only one-on-one time they really got to spend together, because Hank wouldn't set foot within a ten-mile radius of them. It had been nice feeling like she was proud of them, even if they never felt like she actually *saw* them. Choosing to dress up felt different from being forced into it, and even though they still hated it at least their mom was happy and no one was arguing at home. Until the motorcycle incident, at least.

When the day of the dance arrived, Riley snuck out to the barn and uncovered their bike from underneath the tarp. They drove quietly down the back road behind the school, and as soon as they were through the gate and onto the main street they revved the throttle and let it fly. There was nothing quite so thrilling as speeding out of the mountain pass toward town. They parked in a spot on Main Street and wandered around looking for a clothing store.

The ice-cold air of the department store hit them as soon as they opened the door, and Riley was immediately bombarded by the pastel colors of the junior women's dress section. The sight of all of the tulle and taffeta on display overwhelmed them with equal parts nostalgia and nausea. They walked decisively past that section and towards the men's side. Riley's whole body shook as they wandered amongst the racks of formal suits. They didn't know the first thing about buying a suit, but they didn't want to ask for help for fear that the salesperson would misidentify them as some kind of fraud.

The person who approached them, however, wasn't the snooty matron they had expected to see working here. It was Ella. Riley's palms started sweating. They hadn't anticipated running into anyone from school.

"Good to see you again, Riley. Hardly any of the Torrance guys shop here. What can I help you with?"

"Well," Riley answered cautiously. They felt so awkward, but the way she had called them a 'Torrance guy' made them feel warm inside. "I need something for the dance?"

"So you are going after all." Her hazel eyes sparkled. "I think your best bet would be to go with a classic style." She pulled something off of a nearby rack and handed it to them.

"Oh right, classic. Of course." Riley nodded like they had at least some idea of what she was talking about. "Thanks for your help."

Riley hurried into the men's dressing room, sending thanks to the powers that be when no one else was in there already. Only after locking themself in a stall did they take a look at what Ella had picked out for them. It was a beautiful slate-gray suit with a matching vest over a white button-up. They pulled everything on, and when they turned to look in the mirror their breath caught at the sight of their own reflection.

The suit fit perfectly, like it had been made for them. The vest was snug, and acted almost as a second binder. Riley turned sideways and marveled and the seamless way the suit molded to their body. For the first time in their life, they felt like they were truly seeing themself. They never wanted to take it off, but undressed carefully so as not to leave a single wrinkle. When they took it up to the register to purchase, Ella was waiting for them.

"I'll take it," Riley beamed at her. They were slowly warming up to her with every interaction. She seemed genuinely kind, and had saved them hours of agonizing over what to wear.

"Excellent choice." She nodded, ringing them up. Riley passed her their credit card, hoping she wouldn't notice their full name printed on it. If she did, she didn't mention it.

"Hey, Ella?" Riley asked her shyly.

"Yes?" She placed the suit in a protective bag and handed it over to them.

"Do you know where I could buy some hair dye?" Riley had loved the way they looked in a suit, and suddenly the bright green hair just didn't match them anymore.

"Absolutely. Meet me out front in-" she checked the clock- "ten minutes?"

Riley bought a coke from the machine and sat leaning against their motorcycle while they waited for her. Their stomach was still too anxious for them to eat anything, but the bubbly caffeine helped calm the butterflies slightly.

"Nice bike," Ella told them appreciatively when she joined them. She was no longer wearing her nametag and had pulled the rubber band out of her hair.

"Thanks," Riley tensed. More people at school finding out about the bike was not a good thing. "I'm not technically supposed to have it."

"I won't say anything about it. I'm not the goody-goody everyone thinks I am." She lifted her chin defiantly, and Riley liked her even more. "You know, Sebastian has always wanted one of these."

"Oh yeah, he might have mentioned that once or twice." Riley chuckled. They supposed they would have to let him drive it at least once this summer, since he had kept his promise to help them hide it. Their mind started to drift, picturing Sebastian on the bike…

"What about you?" Ella's question interrupted their daydreaming.

"It was an impulse buy. Only I got caught with it and sent here." Riley chuckled, but in the back of their mind they were starting to wonder, had it been fate after all?

"Wow, harsh." Ella laughed with them.

"Tell me about it."

"There's a grocery store around the corner over there. We can get you some hair dye, and maybe some bleach first?"

"Okay, yeah." Riley nodded.

"And this might be totally weird, so feel free to say no if you don't want to, but maybe we could get ready for the dance together? I've never been to one before."

"What about Kate?"

"Oh don't worry, she's here in town getting her hair and make-up professionally done. She won't be back to the dorm room for hours."

"That sounds really great." Riley knew that being alone in their room getting ready for the dance would only fuel their anxiety, so Ella's invitation was actually perfect.

Together they purchased the bleach, hair dye, and some snacks before making their way back to Ella's dorm room. Ella got right to work on Riley's hair, giving them an old t-shirt to wear over their clothes while she expertly distributed the bleach through all of their strands.

"You do this a lot?" Riley asked her.

"I really am blonde," Ella insisted. "My hair just decided to get darker one day and I've never forgiven it."

"No one could ever guess that you dye it."

"I think it would suit you, too. What is your natural color, anyway?"

"My gran called it shite-brindle-brown. Only time I ever heard her curse."

"Is that why you went with neon green then?"

"Oh I went through a lot of colors before that, but I think the green has been my favorite."

"It definitely stands out."

"Anything to annoy the parental unit."

"That bad, huh?"

"My mom's not terrible, she's just…easily distracted. And Hank, her husband, has never liked me."

"That must be really hard." Ella gave their shoulder a squeeze. Riley got up from the chair and offered to curl Ella's hair while they waited for the bleach to set. She accepted gratefully. "My mom died when I was really little, but my dad never remarried. I sometimes wonder if he'd be happier if he found someone new, but honestly I'm glad he hasn't yet. Maybe he will when I leave for college."

"Where are you going?"

"Harvard." Ella grinned.

"I knew it, you *are* a goody-goody!"

"Okay fine, maybe a little."

"I promise not to hold it against you."

"Thanks Riley. Seriously, you have no idea how nice it is to be able to just talk about stuff without feeling…judged."

"Well, I might have some idea. Besides, it's the least I could do, considering I've practically held you hostage all afternoon helping me find clothes and hair dye and everything."

You're gonna look great," she assured them. "Hey, you're really good at this." Ella turned her head this way and that, appreciating the way her ringlets of freshly-curled hair framed her face.

Riley groaned dramatically, setting the curling iron back on the counter. "Too many years of practice."

To Ella's credit, she didn't ask what they meant by that. Their debutante history was too much to get into right now. Riley rinsed the bleach out in the sink. Ella helped them apply a new color and then condition with toner. After that,

Riley touched up Ella's curls with a final coat of hair spray.

"Well, now that we've done each other's hair I think that officially makes us friends." Ella declared, holding her hand out for Riley to shake.

"It's a sacred bond." Riley shook it and they giggled together again. "And if you ever want to talk, about anything at all, please call me." They wrote down the phone number for their dorm room.

"Yeah, I will."

"Good." Riley stood up and grabbed their helmet. "See you tonight?"

"See you tonight." Ella smiled warmly at them as they headed out down the stairs.

Riley felt much lighter as they returned the motorcycle to its hiding spot and walked back to their dorm, suit in hand. Hanging out with Ella

had been exactly what they needed.

Twenty-four

Sebastian

As the Fourth of July Formal approached, Sebastian's terror was steadily overtaking all of his other emotions. What was he thinking? He couldn't go to the dance with Riley, he just couldn't. He wrestled with himself for hours before his dad finally knocked on his door to ask if he was ready to go. He threw on the borrowed tux and rushed out of his room without even glancing in his mirror, cursing his plight that he had to be the one guy whose dad would make sure he definitely showed up to this stupid event.

Sebastian arrived at the dance early, thanks to Dean Otero. The gymnasium had been decorated with red, white, and blue balloons, streamers, and confetti. A cover band was setting up on a stage in one corner, with a buffet table across the way in the other. He aimlessly wandered the mostly-empty room; there was no sign of Riley yet. Jittery energy bubbled under his skin, and he felt ready to bolt at any second. Then he saw Kate enter the room, and approached her just to have something to focus on. Her curly red hair was arranged on top of her head, and dark make-up accentuated her blue eyes. The other guys who were arriving all looked like they wanted to talk to her, but only Sebastian spoke.

"Hey."

"Hey," she responded without meeting his eyes.

"How's it going?"

"Fine, I guess."

They lapsed into silence while more students filed into the gym, dressed in varying degrees of formal-wear.

"Look, Kate I-" he began.

"Ugh, spare me your lame apology about making your friend ask me out for you and then changing your mind." She huffed, looking justifiably annoyed.

"I know, I just wanted to explain..." Sebastian tried again.

"Wow, he looks gorgeous!" Kate suddenly exclaimed. Sebastian spun around, and there was Riley in the doorway. His hair, now a dark silver color that looked almost metallic in the low lighting, had been smoothed down to one side. He was wearing what looked like a brand new suit that fit him to a T. Sebastian felt like the wind had been knocked out of him. But then Riley's eyes met his from across the room, and he could breathe again.

"I had it in my head that I might at least get one dance with him tonight," Kate looked pointedly between Sebastian and Riley. "But I can see now that it's never going to happen."

Her words brought Sebastian back down to earth, and he looked around himself frantically wondering how many other people had seen him openly gawking at Riley. Full panic was taking over now, and the room around him was getting blurry. He glanced back up and saw Riley still watching him. He felt exposed and vulnerable, and his knees turned to jelly. He couldn't do it. He turned and ran the other way.

Sebastian distracted himself at the banquet table, willing his limbs to stop trembling. Why did Riley have such a strong effect on him? What was it about him? It seemed like no matter how hard he tried, he couldn't escape him. And sure enough, when he turned around Riley was walking toward him looking confused.

He felt that familiar pull, and then they were standing face to face before he even realized he'd moved. Riley's green eyes caught his and held him immobilized.

"Hi," he breathed, his voice barely a whisper.

"Hi," Riley echoed. "I was hoping to talk to you."

"Yeah. We should. Talk."

"Maybe we could go somewhere else?" Riley glanced around, and Sebastian felt as if a spell had been lifted from him. The music was suddenly too loud in his ears, and all the people dancing around them seemed to be closing in. He fought to control his breathing, and he was losing.

"I don't think I can do this," he told Riley through clenched teeth, and he forced himself to turn away from Riley once again. Each step that took him farther away felt heavier, required more strength, until by the time he was back at the table he felt like he had run a mile. Why was he fighting this so hard? He was exhausted; he couldn't fight it anymore. He straightened his shoulders and turned back around, only to find that Riley was already on the other side of the room opening the door to the service stairs.

Sebastian's legs propelled him forward, and as he closed the distance the weight of his fear drifted away. He felt lighter and lighter as he bounded up the stairs after Riley, reaching the rooftop a moment later. The stars dominated the deep indigo sky above him, undimmed by city lights or moonlight. It was a new moon tonight, like the night they walked the motorcycle across campus to hide it in the barn. The night that had changed everything. Sebastian stopped to catch his breath, and saw Riley standing with his hands on top of the roof wall and head bowed. He looked so full of sadness that Sebastian wanted to do anything to bring his smile back.

Sebastian didn't think, didn't question, he just rushed forward and took Riley by the shoulders, gently turning him around.

"What are you doing?" Riley asked.

"Giving in to gravity."

And with that, Sebastian placed his hands along Riley's neck and kissed him deeply without reservations. After a split-second of surprise, Riley kissed him back just as passionately, fingertips clawing up his shoulder blades to pull him even closer as their lips moved together.

They kissed until he couldn't breathe, and he never wanted it to end. Feeling Riley's lips on his, his skin under his hands, the smell of his hair, it was more than he could ever have imagined. He pulled away with a gasp, unwilling to break contact but knowing that if he didn't he would never be able to stop.

"Oh wow." Sebastian's voice spilled over with joy as he pressed his forehead against Riley's. "That was…" He had no words for what that was.

"I know," Riley agreed, equally speechless. "I know."

They stood like that for a while, breaths mingling in the night air as the music of the dance thumped far below them. Then Sebastian had to voice the question that had been plaguing him all these weeks.

"But, does this mean that... are we... gay?" As Sebastian said the word out loud, it didn't terrify him quite so much as it had when he was mulling it over in his mind, alone. Something about Riley made him believe that everything would be okay, somehow. As long as they were together.

"I don't know what we are, I only know what I feel. And this feels right. It has from the beginning."

"It has for me too. I just...didn't know how to deal."

"I noticed." Riley laughed, and the sound warmed him from the inside out.

"I'm really sorry that it took me so long to figure this out."

"All that matters is that you're here now," Riley assured him, and then they were kissing again, twining their fingers together.

They kissed until the rest of the world fell away.

Sebastian could have spent the rest of the night kissing Riley, but all of a sudden the sky above them exploded with a resonant boom. Both of their heads snapped upwards, and they gaped in wonder as a shower of sparks rained down all around them. They stared at the shimmering colors in fascination, arms around each other on their rooftop hideaway, watching the fireworks show that felt like it was just for them.

Twenty-five

Riley

Riley lay awake all night, reliving the moment when Sebastian had kissed them over and over. Sebastian had kissed them! It had been beyond anything Riley ever imagined. There was no turning back now. They only wished they knew what Sebastian was thinking right this minute. Did he regret it? Was he having second thoughts?

Most of all, they knew they had to tell him the truth, the whole truth, before they got in too deep. Riley bit at their lower lip, worrying. How would he take it? Would he stay, or would he run again? Unable to stand the unforeseeable outcome, they sat at their desk with

a pen and paper and started to write
him a letter.

Then, as the morning sun was
beginning to creep in through the
window, there came a soft knock at
their door. Riley rushed to find
their binder and throw a sweatshirt
on before opening it to admit
Sebastian. He walked past them into
the room and Riley closed and locked
the door.

"I couldn't sleep," his voice
rasped against the silence of the
early morning hour.

"Me neither," Riley agreed, and
they leaned back against their door
just drinking in the sight of him.
Sebastian approached them, slowly
this time, until he stood so close
they were almost touching, his hand
pressed against the door near their
shoulder. Riley could feel the heat
of his skin and smell the
intoxicating mixture of soap and
detergent and toothpaste that was

uniquely *him*. They were almost the
same height, and their eyes locked
for a long moment as Riley searched
for some clue as to what Sebastian
was feeling now. To their surprise,
they didn't see any regret or remorse
in his deep brown eyes. Instead there
was something darker, something that
pulled at Riley deep inside, and
suddenly they couldn't stand what
little distance remained between
them.

They pressed themself against
him, their mouth searching for his
until they connected. Riley was
soaring again, unable to feel the
floor beneath their feet or the door
at their back, unable to think about
anything other than his hands resting
against the sides of their neck and
his lips moving with theirs. There
was only Sebastian.

But then Sebastian's lips were
moving along their jawline, finding
their earlobe and pulling it in

between his teeth. A flash of heat seared down their spine, and Riley yelped in surprise. Sebastian immediately backed off, putting a little space between them.

"We don't have to do anything you're not ready for," he told them gently. "It's just that, I had been thinking about kissing you for so long, and now that it's finally happening I guess I just got carried away."

"I love that you got carried away, trust me," Riley told him, and the glint in his eyes was almost enough to make them lose all self control. "But Sebastian, there are things you still don't know about me." Riley's head was telling them that they needed to be upfront with him, but their heart was screaming at them to just kiss him until their head shut the hell up.

"I know you." Sebastian shook his head. "I feel like I've known you forever, maybe even longer. Anything else we can figure out as we go along. Right?"

Indecision warred inside of Riley. Now that they finally had him here, right in front of them, they were terrified to lose him. They wanted to hold on to this feeling, and just let themself be happy for once in their life. Was that too much to ask? Sebastian cradled their head in his hands and looked into their eyes.

"Hey, I'm not going anywhere. I promise. I know I ran away from you before, but that's never going to happen again, okay?"

Riley looked into his eyes for a long time, searching for some indication that what he was saying wasn't true.

"Come on," he said finally, taking Riley's hand in his. "I have an idea."

Riley almost laughed aloud as giddy excitement bubbled up inside of them. They would go anywhere he wanted. The campus was still and quiet as Sebastian led Riley out to the barn, keeping hold of their hand for the duration of the walk. Riley marveled at this simple gesture, at how holding hands with him could feel so incredible and so normal at the same time.

The sun had just crested the top of the mountain, bathing the pasture in golden morning light. All six horses flew into a flurry of excitement when they saw Sebastian approaching, nickering and stomping in anticipation of breakfast. Riley hesitated at the gate, but Sebastian didn't let go and tugged them into the barn behind him.

He pulled a bale of hay down from the top of the stack, and used his pocket knife to slice the strings holding it together. It

popped open like a tube of Pillsbury
biscuits. Sebastian then proceeded to
grab large chunks of it and toss it
over the fence to the eagerly
awaiting animals. They all clamored
to be first in line, but a large
brown and white one guarded his pile
from the others. Soon they each had
their own pile to eat from, and the
corral fell into a contented quiet.

When Riley turned back toward
Sebastian, they couldn't help but let
out a full belly laugh at the sight
of him. He was covered in bits of hay
from head to toe.

"What?" He asked, dusting off
the front of his jeans.

"Nothing, you just…," Riley
couldn't stop laughing, "you just
have a little something here." They
reached up and brushed the loose hay
out of his thick black hair. His warm
hand caught theirs, and pressed it to
his cheek. They could feel the light
stubble along his jaw and realized he

had been too distracted to shave before coming to their room this morning. The thought made their pulse race.

"So you've been thinking about it all this time?" Riley asked him.

"Thinking about what?" Sebastian's voice was rough as he spoke.

"About you…and me…kissing?"

"Are you kidding?" He sat down on the bale behind him. "I've barely been able to think about anything else."

"I thought that maybe I had freaked you out or something. You know, when we were here in the barn, with the motorcycle and everything."

"You didn't freak me out, I freaked myself out. I got all up in my head about everything. I thought that if I stayed away from you, these feelings would go away too. I regretted it the second after I told you I needed space."

"And last night?"

"I couldn't keep fighting this, whatever it is." He looked down at his boots. "That was my first kiss, you know."

"Mine too." Riley sat down beside him.

"Seriously?"

"You couldn't tell?" Riley felt their face warming.

"I don't have anything to compare it to, but you definitely seemed to know what you were doing."

"Cool." Riley's blush deepened into a flush of pride.

"What about you? What did you think about last night, I mean."

"Oh yeah, the fireworks were awesome." Riley joked. Sebastian's eyes widened, then he quickly realized Riley was just messing with him.

"Well if it wasn't up to par maybe we need to practice more,"

Sebastian suggested, to which Riley heartily agreed.

By the time the horses had finished eating and started milling about, Riley and Sebastian were once again out of breath with swollen lips.

"You were right," Riley admitted. "Practice does make perfect."

"I don't know," Sebastian shook his head. "I still see room for improvement." He leaned in again, but Riley stopped him with a hand on his chest.

"I have to tell you something," they began. Sebastian picked up on their serious tone and sat up straight, looking tense. "I…I…" Riley couldn't seem to force the words out. "I need to take this slowly."

"Oh." Sebastian's eyebrows shot up. "Yeah, of course. Whatever you need."

"You're amazing, you know that?" Riley smiled, momentarily relieved. It was true, what they had said, it just wasn't the whole truth.

"You might have to keep reminding me." Sebastian cleared his throat and made a show of struggling to stand up. Riley laughed and helped pull him up. "Now, are you ready for my idea?"

"You mean this whole excursion wasn't just a ruse to get me out here alone?" Riley feigned surprise.

"Not at first, but I'm not complaining." He grinned at them. "Come on."

Sebastian grabbed some gear from the supply closet and walked back out to the gate. He opened it and walked into the pen with the horses. Riley held their breath, but the horses completely ignored him, still searching the ground for any tiny morsel that may have been left behind. He walked right up to the big

brown and white one, and fastened a
halter around its head. Riley had
watched enough polo practices by now
to know that these horses were used
to being handled, but they still felt
nervous being in such close proximity
to the large animals.

Sebastian came back through the
gate, bringing the horse with him.
"This is Pilot." He tied the lead
rope to the hitching rail out in
front of the barn, then handed a
round bumpy piece of rubber to Riley.
They looked at him, dumbfounded.

"That's a curry comb."
Sebastian laughed. "You brush him in
circles with it."

"Brush him?"

"Like this." Sebastian stood
behind them, his large calloused hand
covering Riley's, and began moving
the curry in slow circles against the
horse's side. The length of his arm
was pressed along theirs, his chest
against their shoulder blade, and

Riley's brain short-circuited. "See how it brings up all the dirt?"

"You have a very strange idea of a hobby." Riley did their best to keep their voice steady. When Sebastian let go of their hand, Riley continued doing the circles. "Haven't you ever heard of T.V.?"

"Give it a chance, will you?" Sebastian rolled his eyes. They went through each brush in the tote, Sebastian explaining its function and how to apply it. By the time they were done Pilot was gleaming, and about to fall asleep.

"Did you give him some kinda sedative?"

"Grooming is very relaxing for horses," Sebastian explained. "It's like a massage. You should try it sometime, maybe then you won't be so grumpy in the morning."

Riley chucked their brush at him but he ducked it nimbly. "I've had my fill of excess pampering thank you very much." They secretly thought Pilot would be much happier back with his friends rolling in the dirt. "How do you know so much about horses?"

"I had to learn on the job. When my dad and I first moved here they were going to sell them all after it got too expensive to take care of them. So I volunteered to do it for free." He shrugged like it was no big deal. "Ready for phase two?"

"There's more?" Riley groaned.

"Wow, you're crabby when you don't get any sleep."

"Yeah, well, it's your fault."

"Happy to take credit." Sebastian grinned and Riley glared at him. How could anyone be this chipper so early? "Here you go." He untied the rope and handed it to Riley, who immediately tensed up.

"What am I supposed to do with this?" they demanded wildly. Pilot's ears flicked back and forth at the sound of their screech.

"First of all, stay calm. Horses can sense fear."

"Oh great, now I'm really calm." Riley glanced sideways at the animal standing next to them.

"Now start walking and Pilot will follow you."

"Do I want him to follow me?"

"Yes, you do." Sebastian came to stand next to them. His warmth had an instant calming effect on Riley. "Leading a horse is all about trust. You're trusting him not to trample over you, and he's trusting you not to lead him into any danger." Sebastian was looking deep into their eyes, and Riley suddenly had a feeling they weren't talking about the horse anymore.

"So, I just have to trust him?"

"You just have to trust him."

Riley took a deep breath, and then took a step forward.

Twenty-six

Sebastian

There was no school on Monday thanks to the holiday weekend, so Sebastian decided to take advantage of the extra time and called the team together for an impromptu polo practice out in the arena. He organized a three-on-three scrimmage and had them all rotating through positions. When he felt like they were working together pretty seamlessly, he switched it up and set out an obstacle course for them.

"Last one through has to muck all the stalls!" Sebastian called out as he guided Pilot through a series of cones, barrels, and poles. He could hear the rest of the team thundering behind him, occasionally going too fast and knocking something over. The final challenge was a barrel full of water guns. As the first one to reach it, Sebastian grabbed two and whirled around to start shooting at everyone coming up behind him. His aim was pretty good, and their cries of surprise were the best reward he could have hoped for. Soon they all had pistols in hand, steering their horses with their legs as they chased each other around the arena in an all-out battle.

When the water ran out, Tyler, Adam, and Jon got to work on mucking while Sebastian, Ben, and Scott started hosing down all six sweaty horses. Whenever anyone came within range of where the horses were tied to be washed, whoever had the hose would spray it at him until he ran far enough away. By the time everything was done, they were all soaked from head to toe and laughing so hard their sides ached.

As predicted, once the horses were released back into their pen they all got down and started rolling in the dirt, grunting happily as their freshly washed coats became caked in mud.

"Every time," Sebastian muttered to himself, shaking his head. He waved to the guys as they headed back toward school, then carried the remaining horse bathing supplies back into the barn to be put away. To his surprise, Riley was sitting there on the hay bales, headphones on and reading a computer science magazine. He hadn't seen him come in, so he snuck around behind him with the intention of surprising him.

"I could smell you from a mile away, you know," Riley quipped without looking up, voice slightly louder because of the headphones and lips quirked up in a half-smile. Sebastian pulled him into a bear hug anyway, his soaked t-shirt thoroughly dampening Riley's clothes in the process.

"Agh, gross!" Riley protested, squirming away from him. Sebastian snatched

the magazine and stood up on one of the
bales, holding it just out of reach.

"What're you gonna do now?" he
taunted.

"Oh, you're about to find out!" Riley
pulled his headphones off and set them gently
on another bale next to the CD player, then
without warning jumped up and made a wild
grab for the magazine. Sebastian flipped it to
his other hand, then back again as Riley
reached for it. Realizing it wasn't working,
Riley switched tactics. Sebastian cried out in
surprise when Riley's fingertips tickled him
between the ribs, and he dropped his arms
immediately as he fell into a fit of giggles.

"You're not ticklish, are you?" Riley
grinned wickedly and increased his efforts.
Sebastian doubled over, shaking with laughter
as he tried to protect his sides with his
elbows. The bale beneath his feet rocked, and
he started to lose his balance. Before he could
fall backward into the stack, Riley caught him

around the middle and pulled him forward off the bale. With his two feet on solid ground, he stood face-to-face with Riley, who still had both arms around his waist. Their eyes locked, and they both leaned toward each other at the same time, magazine forgotten.

Sebastian let himself drown in the feeling of kissing Riley, giving himself wholly to the sensations, as close together as they could be but never close enough. He was losing himself in the softness of his lips, the smell of his hair. He wasn't going to waste any more time on indecision. Nothing had ever felt so good, or so right, in his entire life.

He moved his hands lightly along Riley's jawline, down his neck to his shoulders. His fingertips traced down Riley's back, then bracketed his hips with his palms.

But suddenly Riley pulled away from him, eyes bright and almost wild.

"What's wrong?" Sebastian asked them, his breath short and feeling like every nerve in his body was singing with electricity. Surely Riley was feeling this same way?

"I just...I...I'm not..." Riley was struggling for both words and breath. Sebastian had never seen him so inarticulate, and felt a little twinge of pride that he was able to have that effect on him.

"Hey Cap, you left a bunch of squeegees out on... the ground." Tyler came bursting into the barn with a bucket full of them, and his mouth fell open when he saw Sebastian and Riley with their arms still around each other. They both jumped apart, Riley grabbing the magazine and holding it up in front of his face while Sebastian rushed forward toward Tyler.

"Thanks man, I'll take care of it." Sebastian took the squeegees from him, and Tyler hurried out of the barn without another word.

As soon as Tyler was gone, Sebastian collapsed onto the bale with a groan. "Do you think he saw?"

"I have no idea. Would it be so bad if he did?"

"Yes! I mean no! Ugh, I don't know," Sebastian wailed, voice muffled as he held his head in his hands.

"Are you ashamed of me?" Riley's question was spoken so quietly that Sebastian felt his heart crack a little.

"Of course not!" he insisted. "It's just that I have to lead this team, and it's a lot of pressure already, and I don't want any of them to start feeling weird around me."

"It'll only be weird if you make it weird," Riley told him, standing up and gathering the CD player and headphones.

Sebastian reached out and grasped Riley's hand, sudden fear gripping him. "Don't go."

"I'll see you tomorrow, Sebastian."

Twenty-seven

Riley

Riley was sitting on the dock, throwing rocks into the pond. There were people all around, enjoying the long weekend, but Riley didn't see or hear anything except their own thoughts. The fear was creeping in again, that desire to run away before anyone got to know the real Riley, the way they had run from every school before this one.

Then they felt a hand on their back and they exhaled, letting some of the fear go. Sebastian was here.

"Hey." They turned to face him, relishing the sight of him there next to them.

"I'm so sorry about before-"

"What are you so afraid of?" Riley asked him point blank.

"I don't know." Sebastian took up some of the rocks Riley had piled beside them and joined in chucking them at the water. He got a few good skips across the pond while Riley waited for him to say more. "I just had this idea in my mind, you know? The perfect summer. I've been watching from the sidelines every year and now it's finally my turn to be a part of it all. Captain the team, win the final match, all of it."

"I'm guessing this grand plan of yours didn't include someone like me." Riley picked at their shoelaces, not meeting his eyes.

"That's the thing, though." Sebastian placed a gentle finger beneath their chin and tilted their face up to look at him. "Everything I thought I would love about this summer, it's nothing compared to the way I feel when I'm with you. From the minute I wake up all I can think about is seeing you again. What I'm trying to say is that this summer has been far from perfect. But it's been infinitely better than perfect because you're here."

Riley closed their eyes as their heart swelled in their chest. Sebastian's words were like kindling just waiting for a spark, but Riley was still hesitant to light the match. "How do I know you're not going to keep freaking out on me every time something happens?"

"Give me a chance to prove it to you," Sebastian pleaded with them. "I promise I can do better, I just need more time."

"Summer's halfway over already." Riley reminded him.

Sebastian took their hand in both of his, tracing circles across their palm with his thumbs. "All the more reason to make the most of it."

Riley's remaining resolve drained as fast as water through a sieve. "Fine, but you're coming with *me* today." They stood up, brandishing their motorcycle keys, and Sebastian's face brightened like it was Christmas morning instead of the Fourth of July.

"Really?" He scrambled up after them. "Do I get to drive?"

"Not a chance."

"You know," Riley drawled as they walked their bike out of the barn. "The back seat of the bike is called the 'bitch pad'."

"Are you saying that whoever sits there becomes your bitch?" Sebastian retorted, grabbing his riding helmet out of its bag and hurrying to catch up.

Riley was shaking their head, a typical sardonic smile on their face. They pulled their helmet on and straddled the bike.

"You're about to find out."
They grinned, patting the seat behind
them coyly.

Sebastian tried not to smile
and failed. He sat astride the 'bitch
pad' behind Riley, leaning forward to
speak into their ear. "We'll just see
about that."

Riley drove them off campus,
enjoying the wind and sun on their
face and the feel of Sebastian's arms
around their waist. They turned east
out of the front gate instead of
west, heading farther up the mountain
away from town. The road serpentined
around the edge of the cliff, and
Riley gunned the engine to hug each
turn. They could feel Sebastian's
chest rumbling with laughter against
their back, though any words he tried
to whisper in their ear were
instantly swept away.

When they reached the crest,
Riley parked the bike and they both
stood up and stretched. The wind up

here was cold and tore at their skin,
even on the blistering hot July
afternoon. They walked huddled
together to look out at the view
below. One side of the mountain
dropped away in a sheer cliff, giving
an almost endless view of the New
Mexico landscape. On the western base
of the mountain, sunlight glinted off
of the city of Santa Fe. Below them,
Glorieta lay nestled in the southern
treeline. The town looked even
smaller from all the way up there,
and Torrance Academy a mere dot of
color amidst the dark green trees.
They hiked along the path a ways
until it veered off into the forest.

They found a small clearing,
shady and sheltered from the wind.
They sat down together, listening to
the rustling of the pine needles and
the low hum of the cicadas. Up here
it felt like they were in a
completely different world, just the
two of them. Sebastian pulled a

beat-up Discman out of his baggy shorts' pocket and plugged in his earbuds.

"I know it's super late and probably lame, but I finally figured out a song for that dumb assignment from last week." He handed one of the earbuds to Riley while fitting the other into his own ear. Riley's eyes widened, wondering what song it could possibly be. "And I also realized that we never did get to actually dance at the dance." He stood and held his hand out. "Riley O'Brien, would you please dance with me?"

Riley took his hand, fingers trembling and heart thrumming. Sebastian pulled them to him, right arm around the small of their back and his left hand on their shoulder. Riley held Sebastian the same way, and they fit together like puzzle pieces. Riley rested their head on the top of his shoulder, breathing in the scent of him. Sebastian pressed play, and Third Eye Blind's "Motorcycle Drive By" filled each of their ears as they swayed together to the music.

The melody and lyrics swirled around Riley's mind, mingling with the feel of Sebastian in their arms. His soft hair lightly brushed against their ear and his warm breath ghosted across their neck. They wanted to hold him here forever and never let go. When the song came to an end, Riley felt the silence like an emptiness that left tears in their eyes.

"Hey, are you okay?" Sebastian asked, concerned. Riley scrubbed at their face, embarrassed.

"It's nothing." They pulled the earbud out and handed it back to him. "That song was just…deep."

"I think of you every time I listen to it," Sebastian murmured, and Riley inhaled shakily.

"We should do this more often."

"Dance in the mountains? I completely agree."

"Or just…talk."

"That too." Sebastian pressed his forehead against Riley's, his hands sliding down into the back pockets of their jeans.

"I always want to know what you're thinking."

"Me too," Sebastian echoed. Riley opened their mouth to respond when suddenly Sebastian's stomach let out a loud grumble. They both burst out laughing at that.

"Come on." Riley took a step backward and Sebastian reluctantly pulled his hands out of their pockets. "I'm starving, let's go get something to eat."

"I think that diner where Ben and Scott work is somewhere around here," Sebastian suggested as they walked together back toward the motorcycle.

"Sounds good." Riley pulled their keys out and Sebastian hurried to straddle the bike before they could get on.

"And just what do you think you're doing?" Riley crossed their arms in mock sternness.

"Hop on." He patted the seat behind him much like Riley had done when they first set out.

"Do you even know where we're going?"

"Excuse me, I've been living here for six years. Besides," -Sebastian winked suggestively- "if I get lost you can guide my way."

The double entendre sent a shiver down Riley's spine as they climbed onto the bitch pad behind Sebastian. It was worth it when they saw the look of pure joy on Sebastian's face as he drove the motorcycle a little too fast down the mountain until they arrived at Bella

Vista Diner.

Twenty-eight

Sebastian

Ben and Scott had volunteered to work the holiday for time and a half, and when Sebastian entered the diner he saw both of them behind the counter. Then he noticed Ella sitting on a barstool on the far end of the counter, watching Ben work. He waved to her, then faltered as Riley walked in just a step behind him. This was going to feel like a double date. He swallowed, willing his nerves to settle, then strode forward with the most confidence he could muster and sat beside Ella. Her smile widened when she saw Riley with him.

"Hi 'Basti, hey Riley!" Ella greeted them brightly as Sebastian sat down beside her.

"Oh, do you two know each other?" Ben asked.

"For sure, Ella and I go way back." Riley took the barstool next to Sebastian.

"How did the suit work out?" Ella leaned around Sebastian so she could see Riley better.

"Oh I'd say it had the desired effect." Riley smirked and Sebastian looked back and forth between them, finally putting two-and-two together. "And how was your night?"

"The outcome was quite...favorable." Ella glanced at Ben shyly, a blush brightening her cheeks.

Sebastian stopped listening to their conversation as the implications raced through his mind. Riley got that suit from Ella's store...the suit that had looked so good...and they seemed friendly with each other now. Had they talked about him?

"It's gotta be Hilary," Scott was telling Ben as they cleared dirty glasses from the bar.

"Clinton?" Riley asked, taking a french fry from the basket in front of Sebastian.

"Swank," Ben clarified.

"Oh of course," Ella said, rolling her eyes with a sidelong glance at Riley. "Hot."

"See, I told you!" Scott grinned triumphantly at Ben.

"Wait, you think Hilary Swank is hot?" Ben asked Ella, leaning toward her with both elbows on the counter.

"Come on, I have two eyes," Ella told him, and the two soon became lost in their own conversation.

"Hey, you okay in there?" Riley waved a hand in front of Sebastian's vacant expression. "I thought you were starving. You haven't even touched your food."

Sebastian promptly shoved half his cheeseburger into his mouth to avoid answering the question. It wasn't that he didn't want Riley and Ella to be friends, he just hadn't been expecting it. He quickly realized the error of his ways when the burger refused to go down and sent him into a loud coughing fit. Riley laughed at him until they both had tears running down their faces.

"Take it easy, Cap." Scott came around and slapped him on the back theatrically. "I'd hate to see you croak before the final match. We'd have to let Tyler be in charge."

"Not a chance in hell, don't worry," Sebastian assured him when he could breathe again.

A short girl with dark purple hair entered the diner and joined them. "Oh my god, did you guys see the gorgeous Harley sitting out front?" she asked the group.

"No!" Sebastian and Riley answered, in unison and a little too quickly.

"Hey Jessi," Scott wrapped his arms around her waist and bent to kiss her. Sebastian wondered when the two had met.

"These are a couple more Torrance guys, Riley and Sebastian."

"Nice to meet you, Jessi."

"So what have you guys been up to today?" Jessi asked, leaning into Scott's embrace.

"Not much." Sebastian cleared his throat as he shared a glance with Riley.

"The usual." Ben answered at the same time as Sebastian, and everyone busted up laughing.

"Yeah, I'd say that just about covers it." Scott was looking at Jessi as if they were sharing a private joke, and Ben elbowed him in the ribs. Sebastian surmised that he and Riley weren't the only ones who had been able to sneak off campus for some alone time today.

"What?" Riley glanced from Ella to Ben to Scott.

"Nothing!" they all answered together, and everyone broke down laughing again. This was definitely feeling like a triple date now. He tensed, waiting for the fear and nerves to take over. But strangely enough, as Sebastian looked around the room at all of his friends hanging out together, it also felt sort of perfect.

Back at the dorms, Sebastian was barely able to wait until Riley had closed the door before he was kissing him urgently. No matter how much time they spent together, or how many times they made out, it felt like it would never be enough. Riley kissed him back hungrily, and they toppled backwards onto the bed, laughing in between kisses. But, as usual, once they reached a certain point Riley put the brakes on. Sebastian would be feeling frustrated if he wasn't having so much fun just doing what they were doing. He had decided he would wait for Riley to let him know, no matter how long that might take. If their time alone together was any indication, it was going to be worth the wait.

When he had caught his breath, he grabbed a magazine off of Riley's night stand and started flipping through it.

"Do you think the other guys have any idea?" Riley wondered as they lay side by side.

"About us?" Sebastian had been agonizing over the same question all week. "I don't think so. I mean, no one's said anything to me."

"Yeah, you're right. They probably have no idea we're together."

"Did you tell Ella?" Sebastian asked before he could stop himself.

"What?" Riley frowned. "I thought you told her. She heavily implied that I should talk to you before making any plans for the dance."

"She's good," Sebastian leaned back with both hands beneath his head. "But the guys on the team don't know anything. I mean, unless Tyler told them. If he even saw anything."

"Would it bother you if he did see something?"

"I just wish I knew if they'd all be cool about it. I don't want the rest of the summer to be awkward."

"You could try talking to them about it," Riley suggested. "Ben and Scott seem cool."

"They are." Sebastian stared up at the ceiling.

"Or you could just pretend like nothing has changed and hope everything stays exactly the same forever."

Sebastian clocked Riley's acerbic tone, and rolled over to voice his deepest fear aloud. "They'll see me differently."

"You can't control what other people think. I know it can feel like it would be easier to just assimilate so that you don't make anyone else around you uncomfortable." Riley was staring off into the distance, voice quaking. "But that only makes it harder on you in the long run. Trust me."

"I believe you." Sebastian could see that he was speaking from a place of deep pain, and he wished he could do something to ease some of that pain. But how could he help if he didn't even know what had caused it? He opted instead to kiss him again, hoping that would somehow let Riley know that he was on his side. When he pulled away again, Riley's smile was back.

"Maybe one of the guys on the team is hoping we'll break up soon so he can have a shot with you," Riley teased him.

"Oh please," Sebastian scoffed.

"Why not? You're a dreamboat."

"And just what exactly are you implying?"

"Face it, you are a very pretty guy."

"Oh really?" Sebastian rolled on top of Riley and pinned his arms above his head. "Am I pretty now?"

"Very," Riley breathed, all sarcasm gone as Sebastian nibbled his ear.

"And now?"

"Definitely," they moaned, and the sound almost sent him over the edge. He fumbled with the bottom of Riley's shirt, and as usual he stopped him with both hands on his.

Sebastian sat up, exhaling slowly as he looked up at the ceiling and started counting backwards from one hundred.

"I'm sorry," Riley told him, hugging him tightly around the middle and burying his face in his chest.

"S'no problem," he squeaked, and they both erupted into laughter at that. The laughter helped dispel some of the tension, and when he could trust himself to speak Sebastian finally asked what was on his mind.

"You'd tell me if there was something wrong, right?"

Riley's eyes filled with anguish, and he instantly regretted it.

"You can tell me anything, you know that," Sebastian said gently. Riley nodded, but remained silent. Sebastian held him tighter. He would continue to wait.

Twenty-nine

Riley

Riley sat in an over-sized chair in the empty library, reading. They were completely absorbed in their book when they felt a hand gently tug their earlobe. They looked up to see Sebastian walking away from them toward the back of the library. He turned and sent them a wicked grin over his shoulder before disappearing among the stacks. Riley could hardly jump out of the chair fast enough, and hurried to catch up.

They ran down the aisle trying to figure out where he was hiding when a hand reached out and circled their wrist, pulling them close up against the shelves of books.

Sebastian greeted them with a kiss. "Hey you."

"Hey you," Riley kissed him back with ardor.

"Mm, I can't wait to get you alone later."

"Yeah? When?" Riley clutched the front of his shirt and pulled him closer.

"Meet me after class," Sebastian whispered in their ear.

"Ooh, I like the sound of that."

Sebastian kissed them deeply, and then abruptly broke away and left as quickly as he had arrived, leaving Riley breathless.

Riley walked out to the grass by the pond, where class had already started. They were still full of trepidation about their future conversation with Sebastian, but they were also still riding the high they got from being with him. They knew they should have told him the truth right away, but damn a kiss that good could make you forget your own name. They were grinning like an idiot when they sat down on the grass behind the other students, and to their delight, when they glanced over at Sebastian beside them his smile matched theirs.

"Nice of you to join us, boys." Lincoln drawled at them, but Riley couldn't bring themself to care. They spent all of class daydreaming about Sebastian's lips, and his eyes, and his hands…

"Riley!" Lincoln's voice snapped them to attention. Glancing around, they noticed that class was over and the guys were heading toward the barn to get some training in. Riley stood up slowly, brushing dead grass off of their pants, when Lincoln approached them.

"A word please?" he asked them, and Riley started panicking. What was this about? Did he know about Sebastian? "You know, I was really hoping to see you participate more

with the cohort. I never see you
interact with any of the students
other than Sebastian, and you have
yet to finish the obstacle course.
You might want to work on that."

Riley nodded, flooded with
relief. It was just about boot camp.
"Sure thing, Teach."

"You're a really smart kid,
Riley, and a top-notch student."
Lincoln went on. "But Torrance is
about more than just academics. It's
about preparing you for the real
world, and sometimes that means doing
things you don't necessarily want to
do. I expect you to try harder going
forward."

"Understood." Riley executed a
half-ass salute as they gathered
their backpack. They were here to
fulfill their penance for buying the
motorcycle, that was all. They didn't
see the point in getting all invested
in something that was so short-term.

Afterwards, Riley told Sebastian what Lincoln had suggested.

"It would be awesome for you to get more involved." Sebastian brightened immediately. "I can show you the ropes." He winked, and Riley felt their insides turn to jelly.

"As much as I'd love to have more time with you, there's just no way in hell I'm going to be able to even complete the course all the way through, let alone get a good time."

"I bet I could show you a good time," Sebastian wiggled his eyebrows.

"You know what I mean." Riley bit their lower lip, trying in vain to suppress the blush creeping up their neck. "Besides, we only have what, three weeks left? Kinda pointless to start something now when it's all going to be over soon."

Sebastian stopped short, the look on his face inscrutable.

"Are you okay?"

"Is that how you really feel?" he asked quietly.

"What?"

"This is all going to be over soon, so why bother." Sebastian's brown eyes were dark, his jaw clenched.

"Sebastian, I didn't…" Riley took both of his hands in theirs. "I wasn't talking about us."

"Weren't you?" Sebastian's voice sounded strangled. "What's going to happen when the program ends, Riley? We should just quit while we're ahead, before anyone gets hurt."

"No, don't say that." Riley tried to speak around the huge lump forming in their throat.

"I just…I need some time to think." Sebastian squeezed their hands, then turned and walked back toward his house.

Thirty

Sebastian

Sebastian lay on the couch in the common room, wondering how his life had suddenly become ruined. He knew it was his fault, but couldn't explain why he had reacted the way he had. Things were finally going well with Riley, and then he just had to go and make them infinitely worse. What was wrong with him?

"I'm leaving Torrance." Riley's voice came from behind him, cold and distant. The words sent panic racing through him. "You're right, we should quit while we're ahead. So, you don't have to worry about the team finding out anymore. It'll all be over."

Riley strode away down the hall, and Sebastian leapt up to follow him into his room. Riley had his motorcycle jacket slung over his shoulder, and keys in hand. Sebastian shut the door behind himself, leaning back against it for good measure. One word was screaming inside his head- No! Riley wouldn't do that, wouldn't leave him. But then he thought about the way he had reacted to Tyler, the things he had said after that, and realized that yes, he would. And he would have every reason to, unless he did something right now to make it right.

"Riley, don't leave!" he begged. "I don't know what my problem is but-"

"That's the thing, though. You have a problem with this." Riley gestured between the two of them. "You have since the beginning, so I'm out. Problem solved. You can have your perfect summer, and I can get the hell out of here."

"Don't you get it?" Sebastian rushed to close the distance between them. "I don't care about my stupid perfect summer, or the polo match, or any of it." He held both of Riley's hands in his. "I don't want to lose you." He stared into his eyes, willing Riley to believe him. He still saw doubt there, the same doubt that was always just beneath the surface. Would Riley ever truly understand his feelings for him?

"No," Riley shook his head. "You said it yourself, it's not worth it."

Sebastian cursed himself for his stupidity. "Well don't listen to me, I'm an idiot!" And then he saw it, Riley's lips twitched ever so slightly toward a smile at his words. He knew then that he still had a chance.

"Sebastian, I understand if-"

"Will you please just...stay?" He took Riley's face in his hands. "We can figure out what to do after the program ends when we get to it. Right now, I just want to be with you." Sebastian's fingers traced Riley's cheekbones, his lips, as if he could memorize every contour.

"I want to be with you too," Riley hummed into his hands, eyelids closing, and hope surged through him. "But I need a reason to stay." When Riley opened his eyes they looked right into him, pleading with him, challenging him.

Sebastian was free-falling into the depths of that gaze, unable to move, unable to speak. Then Riley's eyes began to darken and he was pulling away from him, head turning aside, hands sliding out of his. He imagined his life without Riley and everything was gray.

"Stay because I love you!" The words tore from his lips, and as soon as he spoke them he knew it was true. He was in love with Riley.

Riley turned back to him with an expression of astonishment that quickly transformed into joy. Sebastian covered

Riley's lips with his, trying to express with his actions everything he couldn't put into words. This kiss went deeper, fueled by the depth of his feelings for Riley. Everything made sense when they were together. Riley belonged here at Torrance, in this room, in his arms. Nothing would ever change that.

Thirty-one

Riley

One thought drowned out all of
Riley's other thoughts, fears, and
doubts: *Sebastian loves me!* Nothing
else seemed important now. But when
they finally stopped kissing long
enough to catch their breath, another
thought crept back in. Riley had to
tell him the truth. No more delays,
no more excuses. He deserved that
much.

"Sebastian, I have to tell you
something." Riley took a deep breath.
It was now or never. Nausea was
beginning to overtake their elation.
What if he stopped loving them? Now
that they knew how it felt to be
loved by him, they couldn't stand the
thought of losing him. They just had
to trust that he loved them for *them*,

and maybe it wouldn't matter. "I just need you to promise not to freak out." They made the request even though they knew that if that was his reaction he wouldn't be able to hide it, promise or no promise.

Sebastian sat down on the bed and took both their hands in his. "What is it? You can tell me."

"Okay." Riley struggled to draw in breath, but couldn't seem to force their lungs to work. The words came out all in one exhaled gasp. "The truth is, actually, I was born female."

Sebastian stared at them, dumbfounded. "What are you talking about?"

"I was born female," they repeated, and their legs collapsed under them so that they ended up sitting next to him on the bed.

"Riley, what are you saying?" His eyes were wide, brows wrinkled in confusion as he tried to make sense of their words. The freak-out was coming, Riley could feel it. Sebastian stood up and crossed the room, putting some distance between them. Riley braced themself for the inevitable, and squeezed their eyes shut while they waited for the emotional explosion. For the words that meant he would be gone forever.

Sebastian paced back and forth, his expression hardening as he absorbed what Riley had told him. "I can't believe you've been lying to me this entire time!" Sebastian flung his arms out for emphasis. Riley didn't respond yet, they knew he had more to say. "All this time, I thought I was...and that you were...why in the world didn't you tell me?"

"I didn't know how to tell you." Riley's voice broke with emotion. "I was afraid."

Sebastian was silent for a long time. "What does this mean for us?"

he finally asked, his brown eyes dark and unreadable.

"I don't know."

"Why go to an all-boys boarding school?"

Riley struggled again to take a deep breath. "I needed to know what it would feel like to be myself. Fully myself, without any restrictions or judgements. So when the registration forms came in the mail I just…checked the other box."

"You thought you'd just try it out? What am I to you, some kind of experiment?"

"No, of course not! You weren't exactly part of the plan. It's not all black and white for me, Sebastian." Riley sighed, their frustration overcoming them. How could they possibly explain something that they didn't even fully understand themself yet? "All I know is that I'm not a girl, and being here at Torrance Boys' - being with *you*- is the first time I've ever felt like *me*. I know it doesn't make sense to you, but I promise, when I'm with you, I am myself. That part was never a lie." They pleaded with him to believe them, even if he couldn't understand.

Thirty-two

Sebastian

Sebastian's mind was a hurricane of conflicting thoughts and emotions. He couldn't make sense of any of it, and wanted it all to just stop. But then Riley asked him a question.

"So do you think I'm, like, some kind of freak?"

The question stopped him short. He searched his feelings, and knew that he could never think that about Riley, no matter what. "No, not at all."

"So, is there any chance...any possibility... that you still like me?"

Sebastian had never seen Riley look so vulnerable, and his anger dissipated instantly. "Of course I still like you! I'm...processing, you know?" He sat back down, and took Riley's hand in his. He looked down at their entwined fingers. It felt exactly the same as it always had, Riley's hand fitting inside of his like a perfect puzzle piece. "Listen, Riley, I meant what I said before. I love you. I'm in love with you, and you're my best friend, okay? So just, give me a chance to adjust."

Riley's face crumpled in relief, and he took a huge breath in. Sebastian pulled him closer and held him until he stopped trembling. He still wasn't able to fully grasp everything that he had learned, but he figured that part would come later. What he felt most of all in that moment was that he *knew* Riley, and in spite of everything, that fact hadn't changed.

He wondered, if he had found out sooner, would he still feel this way? He didn't know the answer, but he was starting to think that maybe Riley had been right to wait until he was sure of his feelings for him. When he had thought Riley was leaving, that he'd never see him again- it was the worst feeling he had ever experienced. Next to that, he felt like he could handle anything else. Now that he knew he loved Riley, he didn't think there was anything about him that he wouldn't love. He hated that he had been lied to, but he thought he understood why Riley had done it.

"Hey Sebastian?"

"Yeah Riley?"

"I just have one more thing to tell you."

Sebastian tensed. He was wrung out, he didn't think he could take even one more revelation. "There's more?"

Riley leaned back to look into his eyes. "I love you, too."

Thirty-three

Sebastian

Sebastian spent the morning riding Pilot all around the grounds. He needed to feel the sun and the wind, hear the beat of his horse's hooves, breathe in the smell of leather and dust and sweat. These were things he knew, things he never had to question.

He had a moment of indescribable joy when Riley said "I love you" back to him. He was euphoric knowing that the most incredible person he had ever met felt the same way about him. But ever since Riley's revelation, Sebastian found himself questioning his own judgement. He replayed every moment he had spent with Riley, wondering if there were signs he had missed along the way. He began to scrutinize everything about himself as well. Was he really gay? How was he supposed to figure it out when everything was so nebulous?

Pilot walked leisurely while Sebastian mulled things over, letting him find his own way back to the corral. When they rode past the arena and turned up the road to the barn, he was surprised to see Riley there waiting for him. Sebastian's nerves all lit up at the same time as happiness coursed through him, and Pilot started prancing beneath him in response. He slid out of the saddle and smoothed the horse's neck with his hand to calm him.

"Hey, you." All his worries started melting away as he took Riley into his arms for a kiss.

"Thought I'd see if you wanted some help today."

"You? Help in the barn?" Sebastian smirked while he untacked Pilot and started brushing him out.

"Don't sound so shocked." Riley grabbed a curry and joined him. When they were done, Riley took the lead rope and walked the horse confidently out to the corral. Sebastian leaned on the fence, taking in the sight of Riley interacting with the horses. Was there something different about Riley today, or was Sebastian just seeing him differently now?

"I'm not shocked, I'm astounded."

"Oh, someone's been studying for finals," Riley teased after turning Pilot loose and locking the gate. Pilot immediately went for a roll in the dirt, grunting happily before getting back up and shaking himself violently, sending a cloud of dust up toward the bright blue sky. Riley was laughing at the horse's antics, and Sebastian was watching Riley. It wasn't his imagination, there were subtle changes in the way Riley stood beside him: back straight, shoulders squared, a relaxed smile.

"What is it?" Riley noticed him staring and crossed his arms over his chest, hunching as if trying to make himself smaller.

"Why do you do that?" Sebastian asked gently, taking his hands and slowly unwinding his arms back out.

"Do what?"

"Try to hide yourself."

"Sometimes I just...hate the way I look." Riley frowned. "It's hard to explain."

"You don't have to explain anything. For what it's worth, I think you're beautiful. If that's okay. If that word isn't...offensive or...anything." He shook his head in frustration. "I'm not saying this right."

"No, you're saying it perfectly." Riley entwined his fingers with Sebastian's.

It still surprised him that whenever he spent time with Riley, his feelings only continued to grow. Learning the truth should have changed everything, and yet whenever they were together Sebastian only felt warm and happy, like everything was just the way it was supposed to be. He realized that nothing else really mattered- gay, straight, male, female, somewhere in between. He was Sebastian and he loved Riley, end of story. Sebastian put his arms around Riley and kissed him deeply, hoping to transfer this feeling through his lips and his hands.

When Riley kissed him now, all former reticence seemed to have disappeared. Riley's fervor matched his own, and he kissed him back hungrily. Sebastian's lips traced from jawline to neck to collarbone, finding their own way along the lines of Riley's body. Sebastian's arms encircled his waist as he pulled Riley tightly against him.

This time Riley didn't stop him when Sebastian's hands wandered beneath his shirt. Sebastian couldn't get enough of touching Riley. For the first time, he could feel Riley's skin beneath his hands, memorize the contours of muscles now lightly toned from a summer spent in pseudo boot camp. As his fingers traced over shoulder blades and hip bones, it felt like fire was dancing between his skin and Riley's.

Riley's breath came in short little gasps, spurring his desire until he whispered in his ear.

"Not here," Riley told him, but his voice held the promise of *soon*. After one last long kiss, Sebastian sat down on a hay bale, breathing hard. Riley had just tugged his slightly askew shirt back into place when the girls' polo team entered the barn for their practice session. Sebastian greeted them, then he caught Riley's eye and together they burst out laughing at their impeccable timing.

Thirty-four

Riley

Riley finished running their morning laps around the pond, feeling a thousand times lighter now that Sebastian knew the truth. Telling him had been the most terrifying thing they had ever done. Against all the odds, he still seemed to want to be with them. After that, nothing seemed impossible. They were finally living authentically, and with Sebastian by their side they felt like they could conquer anything in the world. Including that damned obstacle course.

They stood staring up at the course while their heart rate returned to normal. They were determined to complete the course at least once all the way through, if only to prove to Sebastian that they were committed to this program for the remainder of the summer. They could keep telling him every day that they were all in, but now it was time to let their actions speak for them.

They stepped carefully from the top of one wooden post to the next until they reached the ladder. Riley grasped the rough-spun rope in both hands, but as usual when they got both of their feet onto the bottom rung it bowed and swayed under their weight. Riley hung on tightly as they lurched from left to right, squeezing their eyes shut until the motion finally stilled. This is where they always got stuck; hanging above the water unable to climb any higher until they gave up and let go.

Their arms were beginning to tremble with the effort of holding on, and Riley knew they were about to fall. But then they heard voices behind them.

"Go O.B.1!"

"You got this!"

Riley's eyes flew open when they heard Scott and Ben cheering them on. They heard the clunk of footsteps quickly hopping from post to post, and then suddenly the ladder stabilized. Ben was holding onto one side for them, with Scott on the other.

"Try again."

"Thanks, guys." Riley inhaled, then reached up with one hand to grasp the rung above their head. They brought their knee up to find the next rung below them with their foot, gaining confidence as they climbed. Now that the ladder wasn't swinging wildly around, they were able to reach the top quite easily. Riley took in the view from the top rung, supported by the strong beam that connected the ladder to the main structure, feeling immensely accomplished. But this was only the first hurdle.

A long rope was hooked to the side of the beam, and Riley knew they had to grab hold of it and swing across to the wooden island in the center of the pond. They took another deep breath, then pulled the rope out of its hook and grasped it as tightly as they could.

There was a moment of freefall, and Riley let out an involuntary shout of excitement as their stomach dropped. Then they reached the vertex and their arms were almost jerked from their sockets. The rope sliced across their palms and Riley let go, hitting the water below with a loud slap. Pain lanced up their back as all the oxygen was forced out of their lungs. There was water in every direction and Riley couldn't tell which way was up.

Then something wrapped around their torso and tugged, hauling Riley

up to the surface coughing and
sputtering. It turned out to be Ben,
swimming toward the shore with one
arm while the other kept Riley
afloat. Scott helped him get Riley
out of the water, and they flopped
onto their back gasping for air. For
the first time they wished they
weren't wearing a binder right at
that moment.

"I think he got the wind
knocked out of him. Riley, are you
okay?" Ben looked concerned until
Riley sat up and nodded.

"Dude, you're supposed to hold
the middle of the rope, not the
bottom of it." Scott shook his head.

"I'll try to remember that next
time," Riley wheezed, and then they
started laughing at their mistake.
Ben and Scott exchanged a look that
seemed like they might be questioning
Riley's sanity, but soon they were
laughing right along.

"What'd I miss?" Sebastian joined them on the grass.

"Just my newly discovered rope swinging skills," Riley answered, and the three of them burst into another laughing fit.

"These Nikes were new, you owe me O'Brien." Ben pulled his sneakers off and dumped the water out of them, shoulders shaking with laughter.

"Yeah, and I finally had the hair just right," Scott did his best to recreate the spikes, but his blond hair just kept flopping back down into his eyes. He shook his head back and forth, sending droplets of water spraying in all directions. Riley, Ben, and Sebastian cried out in protest, jumping to their feet.

Riley looked around at all three of them, comfortably laughing and joking and including Riley in all of it. A warm feeling was blooming in their chest. Scott and Ben didn't have to help them today, and yet they

had both come to their aid, first
with the ladder and then jumping into
the pond after they fell. Riley
didn't know how it had happened, but
it seemed like they were finally
making friends.

"Hey Riley, you left something
in the barn, that's what I was coming
to tell you." Sebastian looked at
them pointedly.

"Oh, right, thanks." Riley bit
down on the inside of their cheek to
keep from smiling.

"Stay out of the water next
time, O'Brien."

"Thanks again guys." Riley
nodded at Ben and Scott before
walking with Sebastian back toward
the barn.

"So, um, why are the three of
you soaking wet?" Sebastian asked as
they walked.

"Another failed attempt at the
obstacle course. Luckily they were
there to pull me out."

"Are you okay?"

"I'm fine. My pride, not so much."

"Hey, at least you're trying."

Riley stopped in front of the barn door and turned to look at Sebastian. "I'm in this for real, Sebastian. I mean it."

"I believe you." Sebastian still looked concerned. "You don't have to risk life and limb to prove anything, you know."

"My limbs are intact." Riley's statement was undercut when they grabbed the door handle and winced, a hiss of pain escaping through their teeth as the metal connected with the fresh rope burn on their palm.

"I knew it, you are hurt!" Sebastian grabbed both of their hands and turned the palms upward to examine them. "Come on."

He pulled them into the barn and began rummaging around in the supply cabinet, returning with a square green tin labeled "bag balm".

"Hold out your hands," he instructed, and Riley hesitantly complied. Sebastian gently applied some ointment to the rope burns, and Riley was surprised to feel their angry skin beginning to calm down almost instantly. It might have been because of some medicinal properties of the balm, or the light yet confident strokes of Sebastian's fingertips across their sensitive palms.

"What is that?"

"It was originally made for treating dry skin on dairy cows," Sebastian smirked. "But don't worry, I use it on the horses all the time too."

"Ew, what?" Riley jerked their hands out of his. "I can't believe you just put cow cream on my hands!"

"Oh, that's not all I use it for."

"Please do not tell me…"

"Why do you think my lips are always so soft?" Sebastian puckered up and leaned toward Riley making kissing noises.

"You are so disgusting!" Riley pushed him away playfully, but not before Sebastian covered their face in kisses that were admittedly very soft.

"Maybe I am, but you're the one who loves me."

"Yep, guess I'm the idiot now." Riley couldn't stop smiling as they kissed him back.

When Riley and Sebastian returned to the dorms, they found Ben, Scott, Adam, and Tyler in the common room. The four of them were discussing ways to get Ben out of a steep gambling debt.

"I can't believe you bet your laptop!" Scott chastised Ben.

"Ballsy," Adam remarked.

"More like reckless," Ben shook his head. "My parents are gonna kill me. But I never lose at beer pong!"

"Until now," Sebastian gibed him in a good-natured way.

"You should just ask for it back," Scott suggested.

"Yeah, Scott's right," Tyler chimed in. "You shouldn't have to pay that jerk-wad."

"Jerk-wad notwithstanding, I lost the bet and I paid for it."

Riley had to respect him for his integrity. "Maybe we can all pitch in and buy it back?"

"With what money?" Scott wondered. "None of us are exactly raking in the cash."

They all fell silent for a moment, contemplating the problem.

"Well, I'm starving," Sebastian said, giving Riley a glance that told them it wasn't food on his mind.

"Oh yeah, me too." Riley said quickly. "You're welcome to borrow my

laptop anytime you need to," they
told Ben. "I owe you one after all."

"And if you want to challenge
that towny to a beer pong rematch,
ask me to be on your team instead of
Tyler." Sebastian joked, and they all
laughed, including Tyler. "But
seriously man, let me know if you
need anything."

"Ditto," Riley agreed.

"Thanks guys," Ben gave each of
them a fist bump as they took their
leave. Riley was feeling the warmth
of camaraderie, something they had
never known before. Their decision to
go to Torrance Boys' was turning out
to be the best one they had ever
made.

As Riley returned to their dorm
room they were feeling lighter and
happier than they ever had in their
life. They still couldn't believe
their good fortune to be here at
Torrance Boys', with someone as
amazing as Sebastian, as well as a

group of guys who were starting to feel like actual friends. They booted up their computer, trying to decide what game they wanted to play, when they saw the new email notification. Curious, they opened their email account to find that it was from their mom. They hadn't heard from her all summer.

Riley-Anne,

Hi honey, I'm glad you've been settling in at Torrance, I really think it's good for you to start thinking about and preparing for your future. I have some news, I hope we can talk when I come up for your graduation ceremony next weekend. See you soon!

Love, Mom

The shaky reality they had been building here was suddenly crumbling beneath their feet. They hadn't thought this through far enough. There was going to be a graduation ceremony. Here. Their mom was coming *here*.

Thirty-five

Riley

After that, Riley couldn't seem to stop thinking about their mom. It had been a long time since they had spoken, and while Riley usually preferred it that way, every now and then that deep ache, that longing for family, would sneak up on them. So much had changed since they first arrived at Torrance Academy that Riley hardly recognized themself anymore. Would their mom recognize them? More importantly, would she finally *see* them?

There was only one person they could talk to about this. Riley raced at top speed down the stairs to the common room, flopped onto the couch next to Sebastian, and tried to catch their breath.

"What's wrong?" Sebastian switched off the T.V.

"My mom's coming to graduation."

"Is…that a bad thing?"

"She thinks I go to Torrance *Girls*." Riley pointed out, starting to hyperventilate. "After all this time she suddenly takes an interest in me? Now?"

"It's okay. I've got you." Sebastian placed both palms on their shoulders and breathed deeply in and out until Riley's breath matched his even rhythm.

"What am I gonna do?" Riley's fear and despair were beginning to take over.

"You're gonna have to talk to her. You know, make her understand. Maybe she'll be okay with it."

"You don't know my mom."

'No, I don't, but I know you. If she loves you, she wants what's best for you."

"That's a pretty big gamble."

"This is your life. If there's anything worth gambling on, it's you, Riley."

Riley gaped at him, completely stunned. They had never thought of it that way.

"So, what is it with your mom?" Sebastian asked.

"She wants me to be someone I'm not."

"That doesn't mean you have to do it."

"Sometimes it's just easier that way." Riley sighed miserably.

"Oh come on, you can't tell me that's easier for you."

"No, you're right, it's not. But it makes *life* easier."

"I think you should just be yourself."

"Sebastian, I've been down that road." Riley shook their head. "She doesn't want to see me for who I am."

They both fell silent, completely at a loss.

Riley spent the rest of the week practicing on the obstacle course and studying for finals with Sebastian. Ben and Scott would join them in the common room to study, sometimes Adam and Tyler too. It usually devolved into a ping pong or pool tournament, but Riley didn't mind. It was a welcome distraction from worrying about their mother's visit. They were confident they had the literature final well in hand. The obstacle course, though, still seemed impossible. Riley wondered what would happen if they just refused to do the course, but then they remembered their promise to Sebastian. They were in this now, no matter the obstacle.

When the last day of school arrived, Riley breezed through their lit final. After they were finished, they glanced over at Sebastian, who gave them a big thumbs-up with a goofy grin. Riley shook their head at him, but couldn't keep their lips from twitching up into a smile. Then Lincoln led all of them out to the pond for their official evaluation on the obstacle course.

"Good afternoon, gentlemen!" Lincoln addressed them as they gathered around him. "There is only one thing keeping you from succeeding today, and that one thing is *you*." They all started grumbling in protest but he ignored them. "Each of you contains both the ability to win, and the ability to prevent yourselves from achieving victory. Yes, victory is within reach! But not just in this one final test. Victory can only truly be achieved when you overcome all of the obstacles that stand in your way. Decide what you want out of life, and then conquer anything that deigns to try and prevent you from reaching it. Once you accomplish that, you won't just be the winner in today's race. You will be winners in life." He took a moment to look each one of them in the eye. "Now let's go win!"

Everyone cheered, and Lincoln took his place in his motorboat circling the obstacle course. As predicted, Ben had managed to answer the most literature questions while running the fastest time on the course, so he was exempt from finals. That didn't stop him from showing up just to gloat as the rest of the guys stretched and jogged in place before the race. When everyone was lined up at the edge of the water, Lincoln blew his whistle and the race was on.

Riley was the last one to reach the rope ladder, but they were able to climb to the top of it without any help. Ahead of them, Tyler flung the rope swing back in Riley's direction. Riley caught it and prepared to leap, holding the middle of the rope this time instead of the end of it. They closed their eyes and leaped off of the ladder, feeling their stomach drop as they swung across the water.

They landed on the main wooden structure with a loud thud, banging elbows and knees painfully. But they couldn't worry about that now. Next came the climbing wall. It started off easy enough, but the higher they climbed the more challenging it became. The tiny hand- and foot-holds became further apart, and Riley had to stretch to reach the next one above them. At one point they felt sure they would be stuck there forever. They couldn't go any further up, and going back down was not an option.

Sweat burned their eyes and salted their lips as Riley clung to the top of the climbing wall, muscles shaking as they strained to keep themself from falling. They were never going to make it. Then a faint chanting reached their ears. They couldn't quite make it out at first, but as it grew louder they began to realize what it was.

"O.B.1! O.B.1!"

The guys were cheering for *them*. Riley's eyes burned for a new reason now, and with renewed vigor they hauled themself up over the edge of the wall to sprawl onto the top of the wooden structure. They had done it.

As much as they wanted to catch their breath and take in the view, there was still one more leg of the obstacle course to complete. With arms that felt like jello, Riley grasped the handle of the zip line and flung themself unceremoniously off the top. Wind whipped through their hair as they flew at top speed toward the dock, where strong arms slowed their momentum before they crashed right into it. It wasn't just

Sebastian; all the guys in their cohort surrounded Riley, clapping them on the back and voicing their congratulations. They didn't know when it had happened, but somewhere along the way they had become part of the team.

"That's what I'm talking about, guys!" Lincoln beamed at all of them. "Fraternity. Brotherhood. These are the bonds that will carry you through the rest of your life. Hold on to them and you will go far." He brought out a box of small trophies and began handing them out. Ben received a shiny gold first place trophy and held it above his head as everyone cheered. Sebastian was given a silver for best team spirit. And last of all, Lincoln handed a bronze trophy to Riley. With wide eyes, they read the inscription on the base. *Most Improved*. Riley didn't have anything to compare this to, being that this

was the first trophy they had ever
earned, but it felt like winning.

Riley couldn't believe it was
finally over. They had actually
completed the course. They met
Sebastian's eyes, giving him an *I
told you I'd do it* look. Sebastian
gazed back, brown eyes so full of
love and pride that Riley's heart
almost ached under the weight of it.
The changes wrought by this one
summer were staggering. If someone
had told them that the day they
opened their registration to Torrance
Academy would change the course of
their life, Riley would have laughed
out loud. But here they were. They
were finally living authentically,
and with Sebastian by their side they

felt like anything was possible.

Thirty-six

Sebastian

Sebastian was still reeling from the fact that his last day at Torrance Academy was coming to an end. He still had the polo match to look forward to tomorrow morning, followed by graduation, but after that his life was a wide open question mark. He was trying to feel excited about finally moving out of this tiny town, starting college and working toward his dreams. But every time his thoughts started down that path they were interrupted by the fact that he would have to say good-bye to Riley on Sunday. He still didn't know what was going to happen between them after school was over, and the idea of going their separate ways hurt too much to even fathom. So he didn't.

Sebastian spent the rest of the day coaching his team through one last practice, and then he and the guys duked it out at the foosball table until late into the night. Even after all of that, Sebastian couldn't go home and go to bed. It would only bring the next day that much closer. Instead he headed out to the garage, grabbing the spare keys out of his dad's office on the way. While wandering amidst the vehicles, breathing in the motor oil and thinking about everything except Riley, an idea suddenly occurred to him.

For what would probably be the last time, Sebastian snuck into the dormitory and let himself into Riley's room. As expected, Riley was still awake, too nervous about tomorrow to sleep. He brandished the keys with a grin, and Riley hurriedly pulled on some sweats and followed him out into the night.

"Sebastian, what-"

"Shhh!" Sebastian silenced him with a quick kiss, then ushered him out across the grounds. The grass was slick with water from the sprinklers, lending its fresh fragrance to the desert night air. Darkness enveloped them as they made their way down to the pond, accompanied by a chorus of frogs. When they reached the dock, Sebastian stepped carefully into Lincoln's motorboat and beckoned Riley to join him.

"From motorcycle repossession to grand theft boating, you really are a juvenile delinquent." Riley teased him.

"Or you've completely corrupted me." Sebastian winked as he put the key in the engine and turned it on. The roar of the motor sent a couple of ducks fleeing into the air, and Sebastian held his breath waiting to see if it had woken anyone up. When no one seemed to be coming out to scold them, Sebastian put the boat into gear and steered it further into the pond.

As the shore fell away behind them, Sebastian pushed the boat a little faster around the obstacle course. He thought about the look on Riley's face when he finally finished the course, and Sebastian tried to catch his eye again to tell him exactly what he had been feeling in that moment. But Riley was looking off into the distance, lost in thought. The silence stretched on, and so many questions were bombarding Sebastian's mind. He wanted to ask Riley what was going to happen after graduation, how he was feeling about everything, what he was planning to say to his mom tomorrow. But none of the words would come out of his mouth. So he cut the engine when they were rounding the course again and just let the boat drift for a minute.

"Did I ever tell you about how I first decided I needed to have a motorcycle?" Sebastian finally asked.

"Actually, no, you never did."

"My dad made me read *The Motorcycle Diaries* when he felt like my Spanish was slipping. I finished it in one night. Just something about the idea of riding out on your own, no destination in mind, only the clothes on your back and the knowledge in your head. He wanted to get to the truth of things, and to change the world."

"Is that what you want, too?"

"Maybe not the changing the world part, but the rest...sounds pretty good to me." Sebastian took a deep breath before continuing. "I think people should always get the truth, even if it's not what they want to hear."

"You're talking about my mom again, aren't you," Riley sighed heavily.

"Look, we're graduating tomorrow, you're about to move out and go to college. If you don't talk to her about this now, then when?"

"Really, Sebastian? Had a lot of heart-to-hearts with your dad lately?"

"That's not the same thing." Sebastian shook his head, frowning.

"Isn't it?"

"Fine, as soon as I figure out who I am, I promise I'll tell him."

"Fair enough." Riley chewed on his lower lip. "Any progress in that area?"

"You're deflecting, but I'll let it slide this time." Sebastian softened, taking Riley's hand in his. "Whenever I *do* manage to figure myself out, you'll be the first to know."

"Good. I look forward to that."

Hope beat within Sebastian's heart. It sounded like Riley still wanted to be with him after this, but he was still too afraid to ask.

"And you'll talk to your mom tomorrow?"

"I'll talk to her."

"About who you are?" Sebastian raised his eyebrows pointedly.

"Ugh, you are way too pedantic for the middle of the night."

"Yeah, but you like it."

"Can't argue with the truth." Riley rewarded him with a wide smile, and the hope in Sebastian's heart grew.

Thirty-seven

Sebastian

The sunlight was just beginning to outline the top of the mountain ridge as Sebastian and the team led the horses out of the barn. He had gotten there an hour earlier to make sure that they all had a chance to eat their hay before it was time to start getting them ready for the polo match. The Torrance Girls' team was there as well, and there was plenty of good-natured smack talk being parried back and forth as they all worked together to brush the horses to shining perfection.

Sebastian pulled his team into a huddle far enough away that the girls wouldn't overhear.

"Okay guys, this is what we've been working toward! Adam, Jon, Tyler, you three are up first. Tyler starts in first position, Adam second, Jon third. Feel free to switch it up if you see an opportunity. Keep them guessing, just like we practiced. We've got this!" They all put their hands together in the center of the circle, and when Sebastian counted to three they yelled "Torrance!" and hurried off to get saddled up.

Sebastian was just doing final checks on each horse's girth when he saw Riley running toward the barn. Sebastian grimaced at how incredibly late he was, but didn't fail to notice how cute he looked in his brand new Torrance Academy Polo Club shirt.

"Nice of you to join us, O'Brien," he chastised, but couldn't keep a straight face.

"It should be a crime to have to wake up this early," Riley grumbled, eyes still bleary.

"I've been here for two hours already."

"Yeah, well, you're a glutton for punishment."

"Maybe I am," Sebastian grinned. Riley cleared his throat, color rising in his cheeks.

"I'd better go get in place. Good luck?"

He shook his head, still smiling at Riley's discomfiture.

"Break a leg?" Riley tried again.

Sebastian gestured "no" emphatically.

"Good game?"

"That works." He nodded, and Riley lingered for a moment longer. Sebastian ached to kiss him, but the chattering of the crowd all around seemed to hold him rooted to the spot. Finally Riley hurried off to take his place near the centerline of the arena, and Sebastian watched him go wistfully.

When everyone was mounted and in the arena, three from the boys' team facing off against three from the girls', Riley rolled the ball down the centerline to begin the match. Sebastian coached his team from the sidelines, standing on the fence calling out plays. He leaned farther and farther forward while he shouted, as if he could make them move the way he wanted them to by sheer force of will. They played well, but it quickly became apparent that the girls' team was much faster than they were. He would have to think of a way to outmaneuver them.

Before he knew it, the first two chukkers were over and Riley blew the whistle loudly to signal halftime. The riders dismounted and led the horses out of the arena to catch their breath. Sebastian high-fived them as he brought water to the horses, and they all huddled together to discuss a strategy for the second half. To his surprise, Riley wandered over and joined them.

"Have you guys tried making your turns sharper to shave off some of your time?"

"The faster the pony is going, the more space they need to turn." Scott replied. "So you always have to give up a little speed if you want to do a sharp turn."

"That's true, but we already know the girls are going to get to the ball before us. What if we check our speed a little earlier, turn sooner and then steal it?" Ben suggested.

"You mean just let them get the right of way to start with?" Jon sounded skeptical.

"Hold up, this might actually work." Sebastian raised his hand to silence them while he thought it through. "Scott, you take first position and see if you can get to the ball before the girls. Ben, keep a close eye on him and if it looks like he's not going to get there, I want you already turning around to try and steal it. If that doesn't work, I'll head up the far side, then angle in and try to ride her off. If I can make a near-side shot, I'll need one of you to be right behind me to pick it up. If I miss the shot, I'll go in closer and try to hook her mallet."

"You comfortable doing a shoulder-check?" Adam asked him.

"It's more aggressive," Tyler added. "They won't be expecting it."

"I'll see if I can get the ball without making contact first, but if we're going to win this thing we have to give it all we've got," Sebastian told them, and Ben and Scott nodded their agreement. "Alright guys, hands in and count of three." Everyone, including Riley, reached one hand into the middle of the huddle.

"3-2-1-Torrance!" They all shouted in unison while flinging their hands up into the air. Scott and Ben headed over to their horses to mount up, while Sebastian pulled Riley off to the side.

"Thanks for the assist back there."

"I didn't do anything," Riley shrugged.

"Sometimes all you need is a new perspective to get people thinking outside of the box."

"You don't even know if it's going to work."

"We're about to find out." Sebastian grinned widely at him, bolstered by the exhilaration of the competition. "You know Riley, I should have told you this way before now, but I'm really glad you joined the polo team."

"Me too," Riley grinned back. "Now, go get 'em tiger?"

"No."

"Attaboy?"

"Shoulda quit while you were ahead." Sebastian tapped Riley's shoulder with the helmet in his hand, then turned and made his way over to the hitching post.

A few minutes later, Sebastian sat astride Pilot in the center of the arena. Ben and Scott were on their horses next to him. The noise of the crowd faded out until all he could hear was the whoosh of Pilot's breath and the stamping of his hooves. Then the whistle sounded in his ears and they were off. The new riders for the girls' team were just as impossibly fast, and got to the ball a beat before Scott. Ben was prepared, already executing a flawless turn on the haunches to change direction and charge after their opponents. But he missed the ball and they soon outdistanced him.

Sebastian and Pilot flew down the far side of the arena at top speed. He began to angle in toward the girl who had control of the ball. She leg-yielded away from him, keeping the ball just out of his reach while Sebastian swung his mallet over Pilot's neck to try for the difficult nearside shot.

He wasn't close enough to hit it, and the girl hurried to knock the ball farther away from him. Sebastian leaned as far into his left stirrup as possible and blocked her mallet with his own. Then before she could pull back and swing again, he tried for the shot a second time. To his astonishment, the mallet connected, sending the ball backward in the opposite direction and right towards Ben.

"Your line!" Sebastian called out to him. This time Ben took control of the ball, gaining the right of way, and with a powerful swing sent it flying through the goalposts. Sebastian whooped, raising his mallet high above his head. Ben rode back toward him, grinning in triumph, and they tapped mallets in cheers.

When the fourth and final chukka began, the girls were now on high-alert. They began utilizing more defensive maneuvers, sacrificing some of their speed but maintaining control of the ball. Sebastian could see that Scott was getting frustrated when his shot was blocked yet again, so he gave him a nod that said to go ahead with plan C. He moved Pilot up into a defensive position, keeping himself in front of the opposition and clearing the way for Scott. Scott took off after the lead horse, angling in toward her the same way Sebastian had done. But she wasn't giving up any ground this time, keeping close on the ball as he approached. Scott came up alongside her and bumped his horse's left shoulder into her horse's right. She lost her balance just enough to need to raise her mallet up a fraction to compensate, and Scott took the opportunity to steal the ball.

"Your line!" The ball came soaring right toward him, and Sebastian had to spin Pilot around quickly to follow its trajectory. The horse moved like an extension of his body as they raced across the arena, Sebastian tapping the ball with his mallet to keep it going the right way while Pilot dodged around the opposing team's horses. Ben maneuvered up into the defensive position as Sebastian headed toward the goalposts.

The thundering of Pilot's hooves matched the pounding of Sebastian's heart beat for beat as they closed in on the goal.

Out of the corner of his eye, Sebastian spotted one of the girls galloping up along his right side. She was going to try to ride him off. He squinted toward the goal. It was still a ways off, but with only seconds left on the clock it was now or never. He pulled his right arm back and swung at the ball with all his might. It connected with a resounding crack, and the ball sailed toward the goal. Sebastian held his breath as he watched it fly, hoping against hope that his aim was true. It fell squarely in between the goalposts a split-second before the final whistle, and the crowd roared.

Sebastian stood in his stirrups, arms raised above his head while his team was announced as the winner. This feeling was unparalleled, like he was flying and falling at the same time. Ben and Scott appeared on either side of him, raising their mallets up into the air to join Sebastian's in victory. Pilot had given it his all, and when Sebastian sat back down he threw his arms around the horse's neck in gratitude as they exited the arena. The team members on the sidelines had erupted into a frenzy of cheering, and Riley was caught up in their midst. Riley looked so mystified as to what was happening, Sebastian couldn't help but laugh. He swung down from the saddle and ran to him, pulling him into a hug and swinging him around.

"You did it!" Riley crowed. "You won!"

"We all won," Sebastian insisted. "Including you, hacker." His lips found Riley's, pouring all of his exhilaration and joy into the kiss.

"God you guys, get a room already!" Ben teased, and Sebastian froze. He had just kissed Riley in front of everyone. Heat flooded his face while his veins turned to ice.

"You knew?"

"Ben may be self-centered," Scott chimed in, "but he's not blind."

"You're the one who didn't believe me at first!" Ben shot back.

"Excuse me, but *I'm* the one who pointed it out to *you*." Scott rolled his eyes. "Of course we knew. You guys are so obvious. Plus, you both turned down the chance to date the hottest girl on campus, so..."

"Anyway, we're glad you're finally official or whatever." Ben told them with a genuine smile.

"Yeah, it's about time!" Scott added.

They knew. They had known for a while and hadn't treated him any differently. Sebastian's throat felt tight as he looked around at all of his friends celebrating with him - celebrating him and Riley. This summer didn't look anything at all like what he had imagined it would, but it had truly been perfect after all.

Thirty-eight

Riley

Riley felt like they were floating as they returned to their dorm room after showering. Sebastian had kissed them, out in the open without hesitation. And the world hadn't come crashing down around them. But as they got inside, reality began setting in. Their mom was coming today. Panic started building up inside them like the storm clouds that were forming on the horizon.

Riley paced their room, wearing a track into the gray carpet. They still had no idea how they were going to manage today. The thought of their mom being in the same place with them and all of their friends filled them with terror. Depending on what they decided, either their friends would see them dressed up as a girl, or their mom would see them dressed like a boy. They felt tears of frustration prick their eyes. Why couldn't they ever just be Riley dressed as themself?

As they were heading out of the dorms they ran into Sebastian.

"Whoa, where's the fire?" he asked, concern etched into his brow.

"My mom's on her way here and I still haven't figured out what to tell her."

"I thought you were going to tell her the truth?"

"I know I should, but…what if she still doesn't accept me?" Riley's voice broke. Saying it out loud made it feel so much worse.

"She's your mom, she loves you no matter what."

"I really hope that's true." Riley crumpled forward into him, soaking in his warmth as he wrapped his arms around them.

"I'm right here, whatever happens," he whispered into their hair.

"Thank you," Riley wished they could bottle up some of his confidence and take it whenever they needed it. He kissed them sweetly, and their worries almost melted away.

The parking lot in front of the main building was filling up with cars as parents arrived on campus ahead of the graduation ceremony. Riley and Sebastian waited in the shade until they saw a shiny red convertible pull up in front of them. They were immensely relieved to see that she was arriving alone, no Hank in sight. Riley wrung their hands as they watched their mother park the car and get out, cell phone held up to her ear as usual.

"I haven't even signed the papers yet! I'll be home tonight, we can talk about it then." She saw

Riley and her scowl turned into a smile. She disconnected the call and hurried over to them. "Riley-Anne! It's so good to see you, baby!"

Maybe Sebastian was right, maybe it was time to talk to her again. Maybe this time it would be different. Their mom squeezed them tightly and Riley relaxed into the hug. This was what they had been craving their whole life, they just wished they didn't have to pretend to be someone else to get it. Riley inhaled the familiar scent of her perfume and their brain was flooded with memories of all the times they had spent together. It wasn't often just the two of them; they hadn't done anything without Hank since Riley's last coming-out ball. The irony was not lost on them. She held Riley at arm's length and looked them over.

Riley tensed, bracing themself for the inevitable wave of

criticisms. Then her cell rang again, and she turned away from them to speak harshly into the phone.

"Don't tell me I'm being unreasonable! We wouldn't be going through this if you hadn't…fine!" She snapped her phone shut, took a deep breath, and then looked back at Riley appraisingly. "Your hair! It's so…what color is that?"

"Oh, um, I dunno, a friend of mine picked it out for me. It was just time for a change."

"I love it, it's much better than that green." Her eyes narrowed as she took in Riley's outfit.

"What?" Riley's face fell. They hadn't known what to wear to meet her, so they were just wearing shorts and a tank top. No binder, and no makeup. They guessed they fell somewhere in the middle between masculine and feminine.

"Nothing!" she replied hurriedly. "I just realized how much

I've missed you. You've never been gone this long before."

"Wasn't like I chose to come here," Riley grumbled under their breath. "But, I've missed you, too."

"I hope you're going to change before the ceremony? These baggy clothes…"

Sebastian cleared his throat loudly then, stepping forward out of the shade with a hand held out to shake. "Hello, welcome to Torrance Academy. I'm Sebastian Otero, the Dean's son. I'm here to take you on a tour of the campus."

"Oh," She beamed at him while Riley raised their eyebrows in his direction. "That sounds lovely." She took his arm and the tension between her and Riley ebbed. "So, Sebastian, tell me about the college immersion program."

Sebastian was really turning on the charm, and they had never seen this side of him before. They started

walking and Riley just watched them
for a while, feeling strangely
comforted by the sight of their mom
and Sebastian getting along already.

They concluded the tour of the
grounds and walked back to her car.
Riley was still lagging behind, lost
in thought. They were so grateful
Sebastian had stepped in to act as a
buffer and give them a moment to sort
through their feelings. Seeing their
mom again, seeing her *here*, felt
surreal on a completely new level.

"Thank you again," she said as
her phone buzzed once more in her
purse. To her credit, she had only
answered *some* of the calls she had
received during their tour.

"No problem. It was very nice
to meet you Mrs-"

"Julia," she insisted.

"Julia."

"It was nice to meet you too,"
Julia told him. "Riley-Anne, I still
haven't seen your dorm room. Why

don't we let Sebastian get back to whatever he'd rather be doing and you show me where you've been living all summer? Then I can help you get ready for tonight's ceremony, do your hair and make-up. It'll be just like old times."

Riley gulped. Their mom was smiling wistfully at them, and part of them wanted to say yes just to keep this feeling for a little while longer. But now that they knew what it felt like to live as themself, fully and completely, they knew they could never go back to the way things were before. Sebastian had been right. It was time to tell her the truth.

"How about we just grab some coffee and talk for a bit?" Riley suggested hopefully. They glanced at Sebastian with a meaningful look, and he nodded in understanding.

"I'll let you two catch up. See you both this evening." He walked back toward the main building, glancing over his shoulder once more before going inside.

"What a nice young man," Julia whispered to Riley as they watched him go.

"Yeah, he's pretty great," Riley agreed, unable to hide their smile.

"How long have you two been dating?"

"Mom!" Riley flushed from head to toe.

"I can't ask a legitimate question?" Julia pouted. "You're always so secretive, I never know what's going on with you."

"That's because you never listen even when I do tell you."

"I realize that we have a history of not understanding each other. I'm willing to work on that, but I need you to at least meet me in the middle here."

Riley took a deep breath. This was it. "Mom, I…" they wanted to tell her about Torrance Boys' Academy but the words wouldn't come out.

"Oh shoot, honey, I almost forgot the parents' luncheon is about to start." Julia pulled a brochure out of her purse and double-checked the time. "It won't take more than an hour, and then we can catch up. Sound good?"

"Yes, good, I'll see you after." Riley gave her another quick hug and pointed her toward the main building, relieved to have been given a little extra time.

They didn't know what they could possibly figure out in an hour, but they had to do something. Panic and indecision warred inside them as they watched her walk away. Should they tell her the truth and hope she would understand, or keep pretending to be someone entirely different in order to avoid another fight about it?

Not knowing what else to do, Riley fled into the girls' dormitory. They found Ella's door and knocked, fervently hoping she would be there. Unfortunately, Kate answered.

"Riley! Hi." She smiled as she opened the door wider to let them in. Riley stood awkwardly in the middle of the room with no idea what to say. Luckily, Kate talked enough for the both of them. It was a trait of hers they had never fully appreciated until now. "I heard about the polo match and I have to say I wasn't a bit surprised."

"Oh, well, the team has been practicing a lot so, yeah, I'm glad they won."

"Not the win, silly, the kiss! Everyone's been going on about it. I had my suspicions when you were so vague about liking 'someone else', but seeing the way Sebastian reacted to you when you walked into the dance really confirmed it for me. You could have just told me, you know."

"Yeah, I know I should have." Riley conceded. "I'm just terrible at all of this."

"No hard feelings. I'm just glad I got to be front and center for the best gossip we've had all summer!"

"Um, you're welcome?"

"I hope you're here to help Ella get ready for graduation. I absolutely adored what you did with her hair for the formal. For myself, I'm thinking classic waves?"

"Better to go with straight, the graduation cap will smash the curls."

"Oh my god you are so right!"

Riley suddenly felt like they had jumped out of one hellscape and landed in a fresh new one. Luckily Ella returned just in time.

"Hey, Riley!" She dropped her keys and nametag on the counter and shook her blonde hair out of its ponytail.

"Hi!" Riley smiled back, and to their surprise she hugged them in greeting. They had never had the kind of friend who would hug them, and they felt some of their anxiety ease.

"I'm so sorry I missed the polo match this morning," she lamented. "Stupid work schedule. Did you win? Don't tell the other Torrance girls but I was totally rooting for you guys."

"Your secret's safe with me. And yeah, we did win. It was…kind of awesome to see Sebastian in his element."

"I bet it was." She gave them a knowing look.

"Ok, enough about polo, tell her what happened after!"

"Can we go for a walk or something?" Riley asked with a glance back toward Kate.

"Absolutely."

"Fine, be boring, I'm going to find out what's happening after graduation. It is our last night, after all."

Riley and Ella left Kate to her devices and made their way to the girls' dorm common room. It was very similar to one at the boys' dorm, but their pool table had purple felt instead of the standard green. Riley examined it, thinking it might work well for their next hair color.

"What's on your mind, Riley?" Ella asked them after a moment, astute as ever.

"My mom's here for graduation."

"Oh."

"And whenever I'm around her I just feel like I have to be this completely different person in order for her to like me."

"That sounds really hard."

"It's exhausting. Sebastian thinks I should just be myself and that if she loves me she'll accept me. But it's…"

"Scary?"

"Yeah."

Ella was quiet for a moment. "I can't pretend to know what you're going through. But I do know that if my mom was here today, I'd want to spend every minute with her." Her eyes shone.

Riley felt like a world-class jerk. Here they were complaining about how difficult their mom was, when Ella had lost her own mom so long ago.

"Oh god Ella, I'm so sorry. I wasn't thinking."

"It's okay, Riley, promise. I haven't told many people here about my mom, so it feels good to talk to you about her. Most of the time I'm fine, but when big moments come along-"

"Like graduations?"

"Exactly."

"If it helps, I'm here for you anytime you need me. I mean that. Sebastian too."

"I know, that means a lot. I've never been good at the whole friend thing but I think I'm starting to get it."

"I think you're better at it than you realize. I'm really glad that I met you, Ella."

"You too." Ella hugged them again, and Riley felt tears pricking their eyes.

Until a shrill sound broke through the moment.

"Riley-Anne!"

Thirty-nine

Riley

"As soon as the luncheon ended I came right over here to find you." Julia was marching toward them, arms crossed and tight-lipped. "But for some reason the Dean of Torrance Girls' Academy has never heard of you. She was quite concerned when I told her you had just completed the summer program here and she couldn't find a single record of your attendance. Care to explain yourself?"

"Okay, I should probably go." Riley told Ella quietly. The last thing they wanted was to involve her in their mom drama.

"You sure?"

"Yeah, I've got this. I'll see you at graduation."

"Okay, good luck." Ella squeezed their hand and headed back upstairs.

"Why would you lie to me?" Julia demanded. "And spending the entire summer here when you're not actually a student! Did you want to get away from me that badly?" Her face crumpled. "Do you have any idea how difficult these past few months have been for me?"

"Actually no, I don't. Because I haven't heard from you all summer!"

"Just tell me the truth. Please." Her face was so open as she pleaded with them that Riley felt their resolve crumble. They took a deep breath.

"I have been going to school here, but the program I completed wasn't Torrance Girls' Academy. It was Torrance *Boys'*." They held their breath, waiting for her reaction.

Julia gaped at them. "Is this some kind of joke? Some ploy for attention? I thought you had grown out of all of that nonsense. I'm going to have a word with the Dean right this minute! Letting a girl register for the boys' school, honestly…"

"I'm not a girl, Mom. That's what I've been trying to tell you my whole life!"

"Why do you have to be the one who has a problem with being a girl?"

"Don't you think I ask myself that same question every single day?"

"I still think the Dean should be informed about their lack of oversight-"

"Give it a rest, will you?" Riley exhaled, suddenly feeling exhausted. "School is over. The Dean, or anyone else for that matter, never noticed that I wasn't technically supposed to be there. But for the record, neither did you."

Julia's mouth opened and closed, but no sound came out. Then as usual her phone rang. To Riley's astonishment, she pulled it out of her purse to answer it.

"Mom, you promised!"

"I'll just be a minute," Julia flipped it open. "What is it, Hank?"

They walked out of the girls' dorm and slammed the door behind them.

Riley stomped back to the dormitory where they belonged. They didn't slow as they passed the common room, even when their peripheral vision registered Sebastian jumping up from the couch to follow them. He got to Riley's room a few seconds after them.

"What happened?"

"I did it. I told her the truth. Tried to, anyway." Riley paced the room in frustration.

"What did she say?"

"She said she thought I'd grown out of all of this." Their teeth ground together audibly.

"I'm so sorry."

"I knew she wouldn't get it. I never expected her to. But I thought maybe she would at least listen." They laughed bitterly. "I don't know why I thought that. She never has before."

"You needed to tell her, for yourself. The rest is on her."

"At least it's over with." Riley sighed.

"It's her loss, you know."

"Yeah, sure."

"I mean it. You're an amazing person, Riley O'Brien, and she's an idiot if she doesn't want to get to know the real you."

"You think so, huh?"

"I know so."

They stood face to face and looked deep into his brown eyes. They always felt like they could tell

exactly what he was thinking just by
looking into his eyes. Right now they
saw the certainty of his conviction,
the constant undercurrent of the love
he felt for them, and deeper still
the pulse of longing. It never ceased
to amaze them every time they were
confronted by the depths of his
feelings for them. They kissed him
fiercely then, as if they could
encapsulate the feeling he gave them
and keep it forever.

Riley had never kissed him this
way before. It was wild and reckless
as they threw themself against him.
Their hands wove into his hair,
tugging gently as their lips moved
faster. Sebastian clutched the back
of Riley's shirt, hitching it up to
feel the skin at the small of their
back. Riley gasped at the contact,
breaking the kiss. They stepped back
for a moment and just looked at him.
His short black hair was mussed,
sticking out in all directions where

Riley's fingers had pulled on it. Brown eyes glinted as he smiled devilishly at them, obviously proud of the effect he had on them.

Then, slowly, Riley reached for Sebastian's shirt and slipped their hands underneath. Their fingers skimmed the top of his shorts. Their palms traced the smooth plane of his stomach, over his defined hip flexors and up to his chest muscles. Sebastian stood still, eyes closing and breath quickening as Riley lifted his shirt up over his head and dropped it onto the floor.

With a shaky exhale, Riley removed their own shirt, then guided both of Sebastian's hands to their waist. His eyes flew open, pupils expanding as he took in the sight of them.

"I've never done this before." Riley admitted quietly.

"Neither have I," Sebastian responded. Riley's nerves were like live wires beneath their skin as they stood before him, bare and open. But seeing only love and desire in his eyes, their fear melted away.

Riley nodded, and then he was kissing them again. Together they fell onto the bed, touching, exploring, taking their time. And then, to Riley's utter disbelief and vexation, there was a loud knocking on the door.

"Hey O-B-1!" a voice called out. "Purgatory's over, come on, let's do this!" They pounded the door again, and Riley heard the sound of many feet running down the hall.

"The graduation!" Riley gasped, clapping a hand to their forehead. They stared at each other for a long moment, catching their breath as mixed emotions flooded them.

Sebastian fell back against the pillow. "We have to go."

"We have to go," they agreed, and Sebastian was looking at them with such an expression of comical indecision that Riley had to laugh.

"And we'll continue this later?" he asked, kissing them lightly before standing to grab his shirt.

"Oh definitely." Riley nodded. "You remember what they say about practice."

"That it makes perfect?"

"So we'll just have to keep practicing, won't we?" Riley arched an eyebrow at him suggestively, thoroughly enjoying the reaction it elicited from him as he struggled to pull his shirt back on. Riley leaned close to the mirror as they smoothed their hair back into place. Looking at their reflection reminded them of just how much they finally looked the way they wanted, and they were determined now that they would never go back to the way things were before, no matter what happened after this. Sebastian stood behind them, checking to make sure he also looked presentable.

"It is wise to practice before attempting any athletic endeavor." Sebastian murmured in their ear, then together they headed out the door before all their willpower deserted them.

The graduation ceremony flew by in a blur. Riley accepted their certificate in a daze, and then turned to watch Sebastian accept his right behind them. The grin on his face could light up an entire stadium. When he joined them on the other side of the stage, the joy coming off of him in waves was almost palpable.

"We did it!" he exclaimed, and squeezed Riley's hand discreetly as he took his place beside them. Scott Carter and Adam Garcia, were already there to welcome them to the ranks, and together they cheered on all of their friends crossing the stage after them. After Riley and Sebastian walked, Ben Rodriguez joined them followed by Tyler Peterson and then Jon Salas. One by one they high-fived and congratulated each other on surviving the summer, until suddenly Riley found themself surrounded by teammates who had become friends. They couldn't remember ever being able to count so many people as actual friends, rather than casual acquaintances. It was a feeling that warmed them up from the inside out.

Then they looked out across the crowd and saw their mom clapping for them. She actually had tears in her eyes. She looked…proud. Of them, of the Riley standing there right in front of her, not the one she had concocted in her own mind. When the ceremony ended, they swallowed their nerves and approached her. She was fully crying now.

"What's wrong?" Riley asked her.

"I was just trying to remember the last time I saw you smile like that. I mean, *really* smile."

"I never thought I'd say this, but I actually liked it here. I have…friends."

"And Sebastian?"

"He's a big part of it, but it's more than that. It's being here as myself. As Riley, not Riley-Anne."

"I still don't think I understand what that means. But I shouldn't have reacted the way I did earlier, either. You were right, I wasn't listening."

"And I…should have told you sooner, about registering for the boys' school," Riley acknowledged.

"Look, we have a history of not communicating with each other."

"Mom-"

"Let me finish, please." She took a breath and squared her

shoulders. "You being gone this summer made me realize how much I don't want to lose you. I don't want to become the family obligation you call once a week and visit once a year because you feel like you have to. I want us to have a real relationship. I'm aware that I am not always the most understanding person. But I *want* to understand, I really do. I want us to spend some time together in Santa Fe, before you have to start school again. We need to...get to know each other."

Riley swallowed the lump in their throat. Did she really mean it? Did she want to get to know them? "But, what about Hank?"

"We're separated." Julia looked down at the ground. "It will just be you and me."

Riley threw their arms around her. "That sounds amazing."

They embraced for a long moment.

"I'm so proud of you Riley-A-"

"It's just Riley, mom," they reminded her gently.

"Okay, okay." Julia stepped back, sniffing and wiping her eyes. "It's time for me to listen, and I will. Can you just be a little patient with me?"

"Yeah," Riley answered, a small smile coming back. "I can do that."

"I see it now." Julia continued, always appraising. "You're different."

"I'm not different," Riley disagreed. "I'm just finally...myself." They gestured to their clothes, and to the polo team now carousing on the empty stage. "This is who I've always been. I was just acting before, trying to make things easier."

Julia nodded. "What I mean is...you seem happy. Happier than I've ever seen you. So whatever this is, it's working. I love seeing you happy. I love *you*."

Riley's huge smile returned. They couldn't believe their mom was finally starting to get it, and even more, actually wanted to spend the rest of the summer with them. They hugged her again.

"Well," she said, taking a deep breath. "I guess I'll be seeing you tomorrow for dinner?"

"Yes, you will," Riley agreed as they walked her to her car. They helped her into the convertible and closed the door behind her, when another thought suddenly occurred to them.

"Hey, Mom?"

"What honey?"

"Can I keep the motorcycle?"

"Yes, Riley." Julia laughed, her eyes finally dry. "You can keep the motorcycle."

They hugged one last time and then Riley watched her drive away,

still smiling. It was only when she
was out of sight that Riley realized
they would be leaving Torrance
tomorrow, and tonight would be their
last night with Sebastian.

Forty

Sebastian

Sebastian had just finished getting dressed for the graduation reception and was walking toward the gym when he saw Riley heading in the opposite direction towards the barn. He smoothed his polo shirt over his khakis and followed. The setting sun was obscured by dark clouds that were moving closer, followed by the low rumbling of distant thunder.

When he got there, Riley was leaning against the motorcycle, staring off into the distance. Riley hadn't seen him yet, so he took a moment to just appreciate Riley's long legs, lean muscles and angular features. Finally he cleared his throat, and Riley turned toward him with a huge smile.

It filled Sebastian with joy to see that he affected Riley so much, and he rushed forward to throw his arms around him and swing him around. Riley laughed, demanding half-heartedly to be put down.

"I missed you after graduation," Sebastian told Riley after kissing him soundly.

"I was talking to my mom for a while," Riley explained.

"Everything okay?"

"Actually, yeah, I think it finally is."

"That's so great!" Sebastian kissed him again. Riley didn't elaborate, and Sebastian decided not to press it. Riley would tell him the details if he wanted to. "Well, are you ready to go?"

"Go where?" Riley frowned.

"The graduation reception. I'd totally skip it, but my dad..."

"No, don't skip it. You deserve to celebrate everything you've accomplished this summer. Let me change and I'll meet you there?"

"Sounds good." He kissed him one last time, then made his way back up to the gym.

His father had out-done himself this time. The gymnasium was transformed into something resembling an elegant dining hall, with white linen tablecloths, floral centerpieces, and banquet tables loaded with gourmet food.

"There he is!" As soon as he saw Sebastian enter the room, the Dean approached him with a wide smile and grasped both shoulders with his strong hands. "Congratulations, son, I am so proud of you."

"Thanks, Dad." Sebastian was almost overwhelmed by this uncharacteristic show of affection. Then his father cleared his throat nervously, and Sebastian tensed.

"There's, uh, probably something we should discuss."

"Okay," Sebastian gulped, his mind racing in all directions. Was his mom okay? He had just called her that morning to tell her all about his team's victory, had something happened since then?

"It's about what happened at the polo match."

Sebastian's heart stopped. His dad hadn't been able to attend the match, he was too busy getting everything ready for the parents' luncheon, graduation ceremony and reception. Had he somehow managed to find out about him kissing Riley?

"I heard you were able to turn a longshot into a solid victory! That's quite a feat."

Sebastian exhaled, his legs feeling weak as oxygen began recirculating through him. "Yeah, you know I wasn't sure we were going to be able to pull it off, but I had a great team supporting me."

"That's the mark of a great captain, acknowledging the contributions of his team."

"Thank you Sir."

His father studied him for a long moment, then seemed to come to some decision. "You know, there is very little that goes on on my campus that I'm not apprised of. However, I have been known to overlook things from time to time." He paused, taking his glasses off and cleaning them with a cloth handkerchief before putting them back on. "I hope you know that if there's anything you want to tell me, anything at all, I'm always here."

"Okay," Sebastian swallowed thickly, his eyes burning. "I will."

"Good." He squeezed Sebastian's shoulders again, then continued on his way, greeting parents and graduates with a handshake and an invitation to help themselves to the food. Sebastian watched him for a while, wondering if he was dreaming or if his dad really had just told him he was okay with hearing about his relationship with Riley.

As if reading his mind, Riley arrived at the reception right at that moment. Sebastian's heart did a little flip-flop as he watched Riley approach, wearing his formal suit minus the jacket.

"Hi," he breathed, still amazed that after all this time together Riley could still make him feel weak-in-the-knees with one look.

"Hi," Riley returned, sounding just as nervous as he felt. Standing face-to-face and not being able to touch Riley made him want to all the more.

"My dad's right over there." Sebastian nodded in the direction of the Dean standing with the other faculty members, enjoying the festivities. He leaned in closer, both to keep from being overheard and also as an excuse to breathe in the heady scent of Riley's cologne. "I think he knows about us."

"Really? Was he...I mean, how did he take it?"

"It's hard to tell with him, but he actually seems fine with it."

"Wow." Riley's eyes were round as he glanced back over at the Dean.

"I know, it's not what I expected."

"How are you feeling about everything?"

"Honestly? I've never felt better." He grinned and bent closer still, his lips brushing the ends of Riley's hair. "And I really wish I could kiss you right now."

"Me, too." Riley smirked at him, and Sebastian almost broke down and kissed him right there in front of everyone. "Find me later?"

Sebastian could only nod, not trusting himself to speak as Riley walked away. They both spent the evening laughing and recounting the polo win with the other team members and their parents, drifting from table to table without crossing paths like they were two planets orbiting each other. Their eyes would often meet across the room, and Riley would nod in his direction with a small smile meant just for him every time.

Finally he couldn't stand it any longer. He knew Riley must also be feeling the electric energy between them tonight, and it was now almost physically painful to be near him and not touch him. After checking to make sure his father was still well occupied at the faculty table, Sebastian walked up behind Riley when he had stepped away to get a bite to eat. He reached over Riley's shoulder to grab a plate for himself, hesitating long enough to whisper in his ear.

"You ready to go?"

Riley didn't reply but gave a subtle nod.

"Meet me outside." Sebastian took his food and meandered out of the gym toward the front of the building, trying to look nonchalant. The front doors were propped open for the event, and the promised monsoon had finally arrived. Rain pounded the pavement outside, and a cool refreshing breeze misted in through the doors. Sebastian stood in the doorway leaning against the frame to watch the lightning illuminate the sky.

Finally Riley joined him, looking so dashing in his gray vest over a black button-up. Sebastian felt like all the air had been forced out of his lungs when Riley smiled at him, and he had to remind himself to breathe back in again. Neither of them spoke, they just looked into each other's eyes and laced their fingers together. Riley pressed his forehead against Sebastian's and took a deep breath.

Suddenly Sebastian released one of Riley's hands and grasped the other more tightly. He strode forward with determination, towing Riley along behind him.

"Sebastian, what-"

"Come with me," Sebastian requested, and pulled him out into the deluge. Riley shrieked as the cold rain hit him, but he stopped and turned his face upward to let it wash over him. Then they were both running, slipping and almost falling on the grass in their haste to reach Sebastian's house. He fumbled with the key until finally the lock clicked open and he and Riley tumbled inside, laughing. Sebastian retrieved some towels from the hall closet and they dried off each other's hair, giggling the whole time.

"I've never been inside your house," Riley murmured when they'd both recovered their breath. Sebastian watched Riley slowly make his way around the living room, taking in all of the decor. He was having trouble believing it himself - Riley here, in his house. The happiness he felt was intoxicating, and when Riley stopped to examine the piano he stepped up behind them.

Riley responded to his presence immediately, growing still as he waited to see what Sebastian would do. He leaned in, his breath ghosting across Riley's skin, and gently kissed the back of his neck. Riley's body tensed, breath catching in his throat. Sebastian's lips followed the clean line of Riley's hair until he found an earlobe and took it gently between his teeth.

Riley gasped at the sensation, and that reaction spurred him on. Sebastian wound his arms around Riley's waist until he found the buttons of his vest, undoing them slowly from the bottom and working his way up. When the vest was off, he undid the top button of Riley's shirt and then stopped, kissing the soft skin where Riley's neck met his shoulder.

Slowly, he turned Riley to face him and looked into his eyes. They were a deep green now, dark with desire. Riley looked back at him, still searching, always questioning. He ran his hands along Riley's jaw, down his neck, over his shoulders and then grasped his hands. He met Riley's gaze without hesitation, hoping to convey without words what he knew with certainty: he wanted Riley, all of him, body and soul, and he would never hurt him.

Riley nodded, parting his lips and lifting his chin to kiss him. It was the confirmation he had been waiting for. His lips moved with Riley's, faster and faster as he undid the rest of the buttons.

When Riley's shirt fell open, Sebastian's hands found his waist. He wanted to touch every inch of him. Riley shivered as his fingertips grazed up and down his spine, over his hips, across his stomach, and upward until they stopped, hesitating at the zipper of the chest binder.

"Are you sure?" Sebastian asked, voice husky.

"Take me to your room," Riley answered breathlessly. His hands slipped up Sebastian's chest and over his shoulders to the base of his neck. Riley kissed him insistently, hands grasping his hair to pull him closer, and Sebastian's legs almost buckled. He pulled away, grinning, and led him down the hall to his room.

Riley

Riley didn't take notice of anything about the house, or Sebastian's room, or his bed. All they saw were his deep brown eyes delving into their very soul. All they felt were his hands exploring their body, his lips circling their skin, tender caresses leaving invisible but very permanent

impressions in their flesh. There was
nothing else in the world, only
Sebastian and Riley, and where they
ended and he began they no longer
knew.

Sebastian

The next morning, Sebastian awoke
feeling happier than he had ever thought
possible. Then he rolled over and saw that
Riley was gone. Sebastian knew he had left
sometime in the night, not wanting to get
caught when his dad came home. He wished
they could have woken up side by side, so he
would know that it hadn't all been a dream.
After getting dressed quickly he hurried out
towards the dormitory building. But before he
got there he saw Riley sitting on the bench
out front, twirling his keys around in his
hands. Something wasn't right, and fear

gripped him suddenly when he noticed the motorcycle parked right there in plain view.

Riley stood and looked up at him when he approached, expression anguished.

"What is it? What's wrong?"

"I have to go back to Santa Fe."

"Oh." Sebastian's stomach dropped. "For how long?"

"Until I move down to Socorro for school." Riley bit his bottom lip, looking down at the ground. Sebastian was having trouble pulling enough air into his lungs.

"It's just...time." Riley sighed heavily. "We knew this was coming, Sebastian."

"I know." He ran his hand through his hair. "I know, I just didn't think...I mean last night was-"

"Incredible," Riley cut in, looking into his eyes now. "It was beyond perfect."

"Beyond." Sebastian's heart was fracturing along a fault line. He didn't understand how he could feel so completely happy and yet so painfully sad all at the same time.

Riley buried his face in Sebastian's shoulder and held him tight. He wrapped his arms around Riley as shock washed over him. How could this be happening? How could their time together be ending, just like that?

"We have to do something." Sebastian pulled away from him, pacing the sidewalk in agitation. "I can apply for New Mexico Tech, or you can hack me an identity of someone who already goes there, whatever it takes."

"No, Sebastian," Riley said softly. "No more lying. You were right, you've been right all along. It's time for me to be who I am and stop hiding. And I definitely don't want you to give up on your dream of applying to vet school in four years just so you can be closer to me."

Sebastian sighed heavily. He knew what Riley was saying made sense, but he felt like his heart was clawing its way out of his chest.

"Listen to me." Riley took his hand. "I'm going to miss you so, so much. But, I'm actually excited to be starting college. I know who I am and how I want to live my life. The future used to seem so dark and scary, but now it feels full of possibilities. Besides, Albuquerque is only an hour away from Socorro and...I'm keeping my bike."

"With the way you drive, it won't even take an hour," Sebastian quipped as hope started creeping back in.

Riley barked a laugh. "True."

"When do you have to leave?" he asked with a ragged breath.

Riley looked down at his feet, then picked up a duffel bag from under the bench. "My mom will send up a search party if I don't get home soon," he joked flatly.

"That's not funny." Sebastian was struggling to keep it together.

"Sorry." Riley pressed his forehead against Sebastian's. "Maybe I can drive up next weekend?"

Sebastian crushed Riley against him, breathing in as he fought to keep standing.

"I'm going to hold you to that," he murmured into Riley's hair, willing this moment to last forever. He wasn't ready for it all to be over, for everything to change once again.

"I'll call you when I get in," Riley promised, then kissed him one last time.

"You'd better." Sebastian kissed him again, and again. Finally Riley stepped backward, shaking his head with a sob, and quickly turned away. He buckled his helmet, slid sunglasses on and straddled the motorcycle. Then he looked back at Sebastian once more, revving the engine with a wry smile before heading off onto the road.

Riley

Riley's face was wet with tears as they sped up the ramp to merge onto the freeway toward home. They couldn't believe how much had happened in one summer. They were looking forward to finally spending quality time with their mom, but they had left their heart back at Torrance Academy with Sebastian. They didn't know what was going to happen now, only that they finally had the courage to face anything life could throw at them. Maybe Lincoln had been right all along, maybe it was fate after all. But whatever it was, Riley turned toward Santa Fe and the next chapter in their life knowing they would never be the same again. A smile spread over their face as they gunned the engine faster, racing

forward into the wide open future.

Forty-one

Sebastian

Sebastian pressed his foot harder on the accelerator, the engine of his ancient chevy truck shuddering as it chugged its way up the steep road toward Santa Fe. Finally the terrain leveled out, and twinkling lights came into view. The adobe buildings were adorned with a light dusting of snow, and he felt like he was returning home from a long voyage rather than just his first semester of college. Normally he would stay on I-25 North, skirting past the city until he reached the mountain town of Glorieta. But tonight he had a stop to make.

The parking gods were on his side today, as he found a spot close to the plaza. He only had to walk around the corner, and the gazebo came into view. Holiday lights fanned out from the top of it in every direction, and the walkways were all lined with flickering farolitos. He followed one of the paths up to the steps, where a familiar figure was already waiting for him.

Riley didn't wait for Sebastian to ascend the steps before jumping into his arms. Sebastian caught him just as Riley's lips found his in a bruising, insistent kiss.

"You're late." Riley was grinning from ear to ear when they came up for air.

"There was traffic."

"Your truck is a road hazard." Riley handed him a still-steaming cup of hot chocolate with cinnamon. Sebastian inhaled the aroma, not taking his eyes off of Riley's face. Beneath the Adidas beanie, Sebastian could see that Riley's hair was now a fiery red.

"It's still hot," he observed, taking a tentative sip. "You knew I'd be late."

"I know you," Riley pointed out.

"That's true, you do. But just because I wasn't lucky enough to get to keep a stolen motorcycle-"

"Excuse me, purchased fair and square."

"With stolen money."

"Jackass tax," Riley quipped, and Sebastian snorted.

"Any sign of Mr. Jackass lately?"

"Hank is gone for good. This will be our first Christmas without him. Mom's got the whole house decorated. It looks like the North Pole exploded." Riley gazed at him, eyes shining. "I love it."

"Can't wait to see that," Sebastian smiled back. "My mom gets in tomorrow, she's excited to meet you."

"Me, too." They started ambling along the sidewalk together, arms linked together and sipping their hot chocolate. Christmas music floated out of the shops along the plaza as they walked, and Riley opened a bag of freshly-baked biscochitos for them to share. "How was your lit final?"

"Pretty sure I aced it. I wrote about Faulkner being racist. Ben still hasn't forgiven me."

"He'll get over it." Riley laughed.

"What about your calculus?"

"Oh, turns out I didn't have to take it since I already had all the points I needed. That's why I got up here early."

"You are such a nerd." Sebastian nudged Riley's shoulder with his.

"Takes one to know one." Riley bumped him back.

"Touché." Sebastian tucked a piece of red hair back behind Riley's ear. The crisp air had turned his cheeks pink, and his breath escaped his lips in faint puffs with each laugh. The sight of him never failed to fill Sebastian's heart with joy, no matter how long it had been in between visits. These fleeting, stolen moments were when he felt most alive. Riley's hand in his was like the missing piece he never knew he'd been searching for, and now that he'd found it he never wanted to let go.

"So what do you want to do first," Riley asked as they walked, "dinner or movie? Why do I even ask, of course you want dinner first."

Sebastian raised an eyebrow. "Guess you *do* know me. But how about dinner first and then we skip the movie?"

"Hm, I think that can be arranged." Riley hit him with that knowing smirk, and Sebastian was amazed that he managed to remain standing.

"Then lead the way," Sebastian requested, and he let Riley pull him along the street. Riley had already taken him to places he had never imagined, and there was so much more for them to experience now. Together.

<u>Acknowledgements</u>

To Cieran, my love, my rock, my inspiration:
Without your unwavering encouragement and
enthusiasm this book would not exist.

To Jada, my soul-sibling, my best friend in life and
in books:
Thank you for always being there with advice,
insight, motivation, and randomness.

To Maureen: your help and friendship mean the
world to me.

To my incomparable beta-readers, who went above
and beyond when providing in-depth feedback, I
will be forever grateful: Bennu Bright, Artúr Faye,
Sage Stalker, and Cassandra Yorke.

And to my parents, whose continuous love and
support make everything possible.

Thank You!

About the Author

Avery Bridge lives and writes in the American Southwest. She gains inspiration from the natural beauty of the surrounding desert, mountains, and endless skies. By day she works in the equine therapy industry, providing horse care to the gentle souls who lend their peaceful wisdom to those in need. You will find these settings (and the horses, too) in each of her stories.

As a member of the LGBTQ+ community, Avery is determined to bring more optimistic queer stories into the world for all to enjoy. She hopes you find something in these pages that resonates with you. You can find Avery on her website or on social media, where she loves to discuss all things bookish, life-ish, and everything in between.

www.averybridgeauthor.com